Endorsements

"*The Impressionist* engages our hearts with two stories about two very different men: Adam is angry, lost, confused; Jim Ed is at peace, with healing in his words. Their conversation in the park is anything but small talk. As Jim Ed shares glimpses of his troubled youth and the life-changing nature of love, Adam—and we—must face the truth about ourselves and our desperate need for a Savior."

—LIZ CURTIS HIGGS, *New York Times* bestselling author of *Mine Is the Night*

"*The Impressionist* will take you by surprise. This is more than compelling story, it's an invitation to become real and experience more freedom and joy than you ever have before. Transformation is waiting to be unlocked in these pages!"

—MARGARET FEINBERG, author of *Wonderstruck*

"*The Impressionist* is one of those rare books that tugs on your heartstrings, unveiling things deep within your soul, things you didn't even know were there. Anticipate it and savor it!"

—LARRY J. KOENIG, PH.D., Author of *Smart Discipline* and *Mental Toughness: the Path to Extraordinary Success in Life*

"This is an authentic story of the challenge that most men face in life—to be a victim or a gladiator. It is so compelling that I skipped an NFL playoff game because I could not stop reading. This story will instruct and inspire."

—MICHAEL LYLES M.D., Christian
psychiatrist, author and speaker

"Oh man! Instant movement and immediate 'boy can't we all relate to this!' What a gut check! Powerful, powerful book!"

—GARY L. STEWART, author of
The Most Dangerous Animal of All

"What a story! *The Impressionist* is packed with biblical wisdom and endearing characters. Dr. Clinton's novella will encourage, inspire and challenge you to greatness."

—Pat Williams, Orlando Magic senior vice president,
Author of *Coach Wooden's Greatest Secret*

"Combine the insights of Tim Clinton and the storytelling of Max Davis, and what you get is a wonderfully entertaining glimpse into the very soul of human existence. Adam is an unforgettable character and a great reminder to for each of us to consider what really matters in our own lives."

—MARK GILROY, bestselling author *Cuts Like
a Knife* and *Every Breath You Take*

"Tim Clinton is as rare as they come. After decades of leading, equipping and encouraging countless thousands of Christian counselors, men, women, couples and teens, he has pulled yet another rabbit out of the hat with this story. I am amazed by Tim's creative ability to use fiction to demonstrate the real life internal battles that so many face on their way to becoming the masterpiece God intends them to be. This is a must read for anyone in search of healing and hope!"

—JOE WHITE, bestselling author, speaker
and president of Kanakuk Kamps

"Dr. Tim Clinton's riveting story captures your senses, renders you breathless and renews your commitment to reach your potential in Christ. A master storyteller, Clinton is supremely qualified to mine insightful nuggets from the hearts of struggling believers who re-evaluate human frailties in light of Divine Truth. This book is more valuable than gold for those who hear and believe the lies of the enemy. Simply and unwittingly, Dr. Clinton reminds the reader of a life-altering choice—believe the lies, or embrace the truth and become the masterpiece you are created to be!"

—RICK RIGSBY, PH. D., Ordained Minister,
Motivational Speaker, Author of
Lessons from a Third Grade Dropout

THE
impressionist

BECOMING THE MASTERPIECE
YOU WERE CREATED TO BE

TIM CLINTON
and MAX DAVIS

DESTINY IMAGE® PUBLISHERS, INC.

P.O. Box 310, Shippensburg, PA 17257-0310

"Promoting Inspired Lives."

This book and all other Destiny Image, Revival Press, MercyPlace, Fresh Bread, Destiny Image Fiction, and Treasure House books are available at Christian bookstores and distributors worldwide.

For a U.S. bookstore nearest you, call 1-800-722-6774.

For more information on foreign distributors, call 717-532-3040.

Reach us on the Internet: www.destinyimage.com.

ISBN 13 TP: 978-0-7684-0491-3

ISBN 13 Ebook: 978-0-7684-0492-0

For Worldwide Distribution, Printed in the U.S.A.

1 2 3 4 5 6 7 8 / 18 17 16 15 14

Foreword

Power of a Story

By Karen Kingsbury

I was at the front of a line of reader friends after speaking in Roanoke, VA, at an Extraordinary Women event when a woman stepped up and started crying. "How is Ashley?" she searched my face, completely sincere.

"Ashley?" I blinked. Did I know the woman? Had we met before?

"Yes!" The woman seemed almost frantic. "Ashley Baxter."

I smiled. Ashley Baxter is a character from my Baxter Series. "Well...the stories are fiction. You know that, right?"

The woman hesitated. Her eyes drifted to a spot near the back of the room. "Well," she looked at me again. "I guess I do know that deep inside. I mean, I took her name off the prayer list at church. But still ..." her eyes lit up again. "I was hoping for an update."

This is the power of story.

As a novelist I've seen that sort of thing over and over and over again. God puts a story on my heart and He uses it to touch the hearts of other people. Through story we are teachable. We allow truths to enter through the back door of our hearts. Every now and then the message in a story is so unforgettable it almost becomes real.

Like Ashley Baxter.

Tim Clinton is that sort of storyteller. He has a lifetime of truth about faith and relationships and how God wants us to live. His ministry changes lives for the Lord daily. God is using Tim Clinton to change this culture for Christ on a number of fronts.

But in this—his first novel—he tells you a story.

I'm honored to introduce to you the latest way you can learn from Tim Clinton. Settle in to *The Impressionist* and its beautifully written lessons. Let God speak to you between the lines.

Who knows?

You just might remember the journey forever.

#1 *New York Times* Bestselling novelist Karen Kingsbury is America's Favorite Storyteller. She has nearly 25 million books in print and her last dozen titles have all topped bestseller charts. Karen is also a speaker at Extraordinary Women events around the country. She is a fan of Tim and Julie Clinton and everything they stand for. Karen lives in Nashville, TN., with her husband Don and their five sons, and nearby their daughter, Kelsey, who is married to Christian Recording Artist Kyle Kupecky. You can learn more about Karen Kingsbury at www.KarenKingsbury.com.

Dedicated to James Edward Clinton, who first taught me about the love of God and the truth that is in Christ. A faithful father, husband and pastor extraordinaire, he brought healing to all he encountered, teaching others to become the masterpiece God created us to be.

"*Remember the Lord, great and awesome, and fight for your brethren, your sons, your daughters, your wives, and your houses.*"
—*Nehemiah 4:14*

1

"So what are you trying to say Paige?" My voice began to elevate. "Go ahead. Spit it out! What cha got? I can take it!"

She snapped her head toward me, eyes piercing. "Just forget it Adam, all right. I don't want to fight."

"You don't want to fight?" I laughed. "You started this for crying out loud!" Frustrated, I jerked opened the refrigerator and stared inside while drumming my fingers on the door.

"I hate it when you do that."

"Do what?"

"Stand there with the refrigerator door open. You're letting all the cold air out. Make a decision or close the door."

"You want it shut? Well fine!" I slammed the refrigerator door so hard bottles knocked over inside and several family pictures jarred loose from their magnets and fluttered to the floor. Paige flinched backward, stunned by my outburst.

"That wasn't very smart," she said.

"There you go again!" I shouted. "Criticizing! That's all you do anymore!"

"I wasn't criticizing, just stating a fact. The last thing we need right now is to buy a new refrigerator."

"What's that supposed to mean? You know how hard I work!"

"You?" she said. "I work hard too." Then Paige did what she usually does when she's upset. She started cleaning. I hate it when she does that. She turned on the faucet and began washing our breakfast dishes while staring off into space. I hate that too—when she checks out on me like she wishes she were somewhere else. But don't be fooled, Paige knows exactly what she's doing. She's pushing my buttons. It gives her a sense of power. I moved to her side, looking down on her, violating her personal space, pushing *her* buttons.

"We have a dishwasher you know," I said.

Paige didn't respond, just kept washing.

"Oh, now you're silent?" I barked, pressing. "You know it drives me crazy when you clam up like that—get me all worked up and then shut me out! It's a game to you isn't it?" Giving in to rage, my mouth couldn't stop. I was on a roll, a runaway train out of control. "You're sorry you married me, aren't you? Just admit it! It's true! I know that's what you're thinking—how disappointed you are in me."

"I never said that."

"You don't have to, Paige. It's written all over your face!"

Paige slammed down a plate into the sink shattering it. "Fine," she cried out, "I'm sorry I married you! There, I said it! Happy now?" She turned away from me to gaze out the kitchen window. Wetness formed in the corner of her eyes and her bottom lip began to quiver. "It wasn't supposed to be like—" She cut herself off before finishing the sentence and began carefully picking up the broken pieces of plate and placing them in the trash canister under the sink.

Clutching her shoulder, I spun her around to face me. "What Paige?" I demanded. "It wasn't supposed to be like what?"

She pushed herself away from me, stronger, forcefully. "*This* okay! It wasn't supposed to be like *this!* I can't take *this* anymore! Something's got to change Adam."

"Change!" I yelled back. "What do you mean? ...Oh, you mean me, right? I've got to change?"

"Hey, if the shoe fits!"

"The problem is you're impossible! I can't please you no matter what I do!"

Paige took a moment to regain her composure and then smiled sadly through her pain. "You should take some lessons from Eric," she said calm and calculating. "It's so obvious how much he loves *his* Carolyn."

"Eric?" I shook my head in disbelief. "You gotta be kidding me? The guy's a wuss! And it's not exactly like you're in competition for the World's Greatest Wife Award! Maybe you could take some lessons from Carolyn...maybe join her fitness class. It's definitely working for her!"

The moment those poisonous darts shot out of my mouth, I wished I could have pulled them back. Before my eyes, I watched my wife go limp as the deadly toxin took effect. Then the tears burst free and flowed down her cheeks, her expression no longer of anger but of defeat and devastation, of hurt. Paige collapsed into a kitchen table chair and buried her head into her hands.

"I'm tired Adam," she said through broken sobs. "I've had enough. I want out. I've got to get out."

It took a moment for the full impact of her words to register in my brain. These were words I'd never heard before, words that Paige had never uttered, not in the entire nineteen years of our marriage. Yes, we'd argued before, done the dance, but it had never come to this. This time a line had been crossed. Issues and feelings that had been percolating for years had finally boiled to the surface. Staggering under the weight of her words, a panic began to seize me.

"You don't really mean that," I plead while reaching out to touch her arm. "I'm tired too, honey. We're both worn out. Be reasonable. Let's just talk about this later when we're not upset. I wasn't thinking, just reacting."

"Don't touch me!" She yanked her arm back, recoiling away from me as if she'd been burned. "Leave me alone!"

"All right," I said stepping back gingerly. I leaned against the counter with my arms folded across my chest, not knowing what to do. "If that's what you really want...for now."

"Oh trust me, Adam. It's what I want!" She dabbed her eyes with the dish towel she was holding. "Right now what I want is to be as far away from you as possible!"

Feeling the knife twisting in my gut, out of nowhere, I blurted out desperately. "God hates divorce!"

"Really, Adam?" she spat. "I didn't know that! God also hates husbands being jerks!"

Realizing my mouth had already done way too much damage, I fought the urge to lash out again. Nervously, I shifted my weight from one foot to the other, looking at her. Paige laid her head down on the table and closed her eyes like every bit of energy had been drained from her. An awkward silence filled the kitchen magnifying the everyday sounds around us. Water dripped slowly from the faucet, echoing off the stainless steel sink, while the refrigerator hummed. Birds chirped outside the window and dogs barked in the distance.

"There's something else I need to tell you," Paige eventually said. "The timing stinks, but it's important."

"Fire away," I replied. "It can't get any worse."

"Yes it can," she moaned. "Josh is using again."

"What!" I pounded my fist against the granite countertop. "I thought his tests have been clean?"

"Apparently he's been lying to us. He's been using synthetic marijuana that's undetectable to most tests. They changed tests. The principal called. They also found pills in his locker—Xanax."

"Xanax?"

"Yes, so he's suspended again. They haven't decided if they are going to expel him. The handbook calls for expulsion and he could go to jail, Adam!"

"Ugh...what's wrong with that kid! What happened to my boy?" I said, my rage rising. "He's been playing us this whole time! And you were planning on telling me this when?"

"I didn't call you because I knew how upset you'd get and Josh begged me not to say anything until you got back in town. I was going to tell you first thing this morning but..."

"And you obliged him! I'm your husband, his father!"

"You're never around anyway."

"That's low Paige!" I slammed my heel against the cabinet. "It's all on me, how convenient."

She flinched. "Stop slamming things!"

"You're the one who's always complaining about the money!" I threw my hands up and made a beeline out the kitchen toward Josh's room. "It's past ten and he's still sleeping! Get ready to call 911 cause he's gonna need an ambulance when I'm finished with him!"

Paige jumped up from the table and ran after me. "Adam! STOP!"

Already in the hallway, I turned around. "What now!"

"You're too angry!"

"Oh no, I'm angry," I said. "You wanted me worked up—well you got it!"

"Don't say or do something you'll regret! Please!"

I moved to ignore her.

"I'll call the cops, Adam! I swear I will!" Her eyes locked onto mine, narrowing. Gone were the tears, now replaced with fire, a mother's fire.

Believing her every word, I stopped dead in my tracks only a few feet from Josh's bedroom door contemplating. The simmering rage inside of me was at the point of eruption. With clinched teeth and fists, my temples and neck throbbed. I'd never considered myself a violent person but things were changing fast. At any second I was going to blow and the harm caused from the shrapnel would not be pretty. "Aaaaaaahh-hhh!" I screamed so loudly, I was sure every neighbor on the block could hear it. Blowing past Paige, I bolted out the front door slamming it behind me. With my hands shoved deep into my jean pockets, I exploded on a half-deflated soccer ball that was laying in the front yard. The second it launched from my foot I realized it had become a projectile that could do serious damage to something or someone. Once again, I'd reacted before thinking. Fortunately, the ball arched in the air and across two driveways eventually rolling to a stop underneath a neighbor's minivan. "Safe from at least one law-suit," I mumbled as I stormed down the street.

2

There was a crisp, fall breeze stirring the leaves that Saturday morning. It was a great day to get some air. If my head hadn't been so clouded with anger maybe I could've enjoyed it. Still, I had to get away and driving was out of the question because I'd probably run over somebody! I knew one thing for sure. I didn't want to go back in that house. So I walked. It just so happens that our neighborhood is located about six or so blocks from Indian Mounds City Park. Unusually nice, it's the city's biggest one and a much-needed reprieve from the concrete jungle. It had been one of the perks for us moving to the area. Wearing an old pair of Nike running shoes, my favorite UM sweatshirt, and too upset to do anything else, that's where I headed.

Indian Mounds boasts of numerous paved trails weaving throughout a canopy of trees and gardens with periodic fitness stops along the way. The main trail circles around a tranquil sixty-acre lake complete with an assortment of duck and geese. On any given day a plethora of die-hard fishermen line the banks casting their lines. During the summer months, wind surfers and small sailboats abound. Dotted strategically around the area are playgrounds and picnic tables with barbeque pits. At the park's entrance there's a fifty-foot totem pole overlooking five historical Indian burial mounds, thus the name. Across the boulevard is a convenience store where I stopped to pick up a drink before hitting the trail.

Once inside the store I marched up to the cooler, opened the glass door, and reached for a Dasani but jerked out the Red Bull instead. Yes, that's what suited me at the moment, a triple shot of caffeine! When I spun around to head to the cash register, I ran smack dab into Eric from church. I nearly knocked him over. He was standing right there! I couldn't believe it! What are the odds?

"Hey, Adam," he said beaming like he'd just won the lottery or something. He was dressed to the hilt in running apparel—tight, long-sleeved, dry-fit, fluorescent green shirt, black tights, and high-dollar matching shoes. "How you doing, brother?" he asked. "You okay man?" No doubt he could tell something was up with me. Hiding my emotions has never been one of my strong suits. Still, I put on the best religious face I could.

"Great!" I said, "Couldn't be better." I lied.

"Good to hear." He zeroed in on my Red Bull. "You know that stuff's bad for you?"

"Yep, but the kick is ridiculous!" I said moving to go around him.

"I get my kick from the Lord, brother!"

"I'm happy for you," I mumbled under my breath.

"What's that?"

"Nothing," I said over my shoulder.

"So how are Paige and Josh?" he asked following me, oblivious to my not so subtle hints. "It's been a while since I've seen you guys at church."

"We've been going to the early service." I lied again.

"Well that's the one we go to," he said with a puzzled look. "I should have seen you."

"How's Carolyn?" I asked to change the subject. That was a mistake.

"You know me," he said with a big grin plastered across his face. "I married way out of my league. We're soul mates! The longer I'm married to her, the better it gets." He pulled up a picture of him and Carolyn on his iPhone. "Check it out," he said, shoving it in my face. The two of them were standing on a picturesque beach in Hawaii. She was in a skimpy swimsuit with her arms around him. "Am I the most blessed man alive or what?"

He was lucky all right, though I never could figure what she saw in him. *He's just a total punk,* I thought.

"God's doing so much in our lives," he continued. "And I have to brag on Garrett too. He just got back from his mission trip to Haiti. They provided shoes for over three hundred homeless children. When he got home, he received The Most Dedicated Disciple Award in youth group."

"There's an actual award for that?"

"Yeah man. I'm so proud of him! I mean, with so many kids making poor choices these days. Did you hear about Allie's scholarship?"

"No," I said, but I was quite sure he was going to tell me.

"She got a full ride," he smiled so big the glare from his white teeth made me squint. "She's thinking pre-med."

"That's really great, Eric," I said with as much sincerity as I could muster. Allie and Josh had dated a couple times. He was smitten and she told him she just wanted to be friends. It killed him.

"God is faithful, brother!" said Eric.

I figured maybe they should give Eric The Most Humble Christian Award. He'd hang it on his fireplace mantle so everyone could see it! "Look, Eric," I said agitatedly, "I'd love to chat more, but I really need to take off. Family needs me. You know how it is?"

"Sure do, man! Shortage of fathers these days. I'll look for you guys tomorrow."

"Yeah."

At the counter, Yolanda rang me up—$1.97. I reached into my pocket to pull out my wallet and realized I'd left it at home along with my iPhone. "Crap!" I said. "Left my wallet at the house."

Yolanda smiled back at me compassionately. With that weathered look, I could tell life had not been particularly kind to her. She needed some dental work and crow's feet formed in the corner of her eyes. I could relate. "That's okay baby," she said with a wink. "You just drop back by later and pay. I know how it is."

"Thanks," I said. "I appreciate it."

Behind me, Eric spoke up. "Don't worry about it, brother. I got it!"

"You're the best, Eric," I said wanting to slap that ridiculous grin off his face. I know. I know. I have issues.

While Yolanda took Eric's money, I dashed out the door, through the store parking lot, and hurried across the boulevard to the park before Eric had time to check out and follow me. I supposed he was on his way to the park as well. The last thing I wanted was to talk to him or anyone else for that matter. I just wanted to be left alone.

3

Walking briskly along the trail constantly glancing over my shoulder hoping to evade Eric, my mind reeled with all the things in my life I was disappointed with—my marriage, my son, job, but mostly myself. I was my own worst enemy. *"Just look at you, Adam,"* a voice hissed in my ear. *"You're a pathetic loser. You can't even please your wife. Paige was right. It wasn't supposed to be like this. You surely thought things would be different by now, didn't you? Remember all those big dreams? The great things you were going to do? So, how'd you become...this? Everything's such a struggle isn't it? You're a failure as a father too. And Josh is just like you—a loser."*

As my mind spun and one fitness buff after another zipped past me in their spandex and Reeboks, guilt and shame bore down on me pushing me to the edge of despair. My stomach churned making me feel like I might vomit, so I plopped down on a bench facing the lake to take some deep breaths. While sitting there some ducks waddled up from the water and quacked around my feet begging for food that I didn't possess. I shooed them away with my foot.

"God, are You even there?" I mumbled, taking a long gulp of my Red Bull. "If You are real, You surely can't be 'all powerful' because You made me. What a huge mistake that was." In quiet desperation, I locked my hands behind my head. A beach in the Caribbean strongly appealed to me—not a vacation, but a permanent escape. I've heard about guys who do that. They chuck everything, get a sailboat, and then work at a little beachside resort or something when they're not sailing around the islands. No worries, no dressing up, just shorts, hat, and some flip flops. *Yeah, like that's going to happen.* Closing my eyes, I reasoned if I fell asleep and never woke up, it wouldn't be so bad.

"Don't you get it, Adam?" the voice poked. *"God's not listening to you. He's disappointed in you. Just like Paige. He loathes you—everything about you. Josh hates you too. They'd be better off if you were out of the picture. They wouldn't even miss you. Just admit it. You're a fraud. You've let God down so many times."*

"Shut up!" I yelled crushing my empty Red Bull can in my hand and then flinging it toward a garbage barrel that was several yards off to my side. Clanging against the metal drum, the tin can fell short of the goal, just like so many other things in my life. How many opportunities had I let slip through my fingers? So many things that could have been. When I stood to pick up my litter, an elderly man who I figured to be somewhere in his eighties stepped off the trail from behind me and up to the garbage barrel. "That's okay, friend," he said. "I've got it." He reached down, one hand bracing his back, and picked up my crushed Red Bull can and dropped it into the trash.

"Thanks," I said with an edge.

Straightening up to a good six-two or three, the old gentleman nodded humbly while tipping his white cap with the black and gold New Orleans Saints logo stitched on it. "My pleasure," he said. Oddly, a few feet away from him on the trail, he'd left what appeared to be a small, handmade cart filled with an assortment of painting supplies—brushes, rags, a palette, tubes of paint, rolled-up paper, an umbrella, a collapsible easel and stool, and a plastic jug of water among other necessities. I'd seen the fishermen pull similar carts, but never a painter. Not around here. *Probably got mental issues,* I thought.

"Looks like you've got a lot on your mind," he pressed, stepping closer to me.

"At least you still have your eyesight old man," I shot back at him, glaring. Like I said, I just wanted to be left alone.

He only smiled warmly and rubbed his chin. "Would you perhaps allow me the honor of painting your portrait?" he asked.

"What?" I snapped. "Do I look like I want my picture painted?" *That's why the old coot picked up my can! He saw it as an opportunity to sell me! Clever, but I'm no fool.* "Leave me alone, please! Go paint a duck or something." I thought for certain that my crude remarks would dissuade him, but the old guy simply stood there unfazed. "Are you deaf?"

"I heard you," he said.

"Look, I don't know what your deal is, but you don't want to be anywhere near me right now—seriously!"

He *still* didn't move, just stared at me. The whites of his eyes sat deep in their sockets behind silver-framed bifocals. His milk-chocolate skin enhanced a silver mustache, bushy eyebrows, and silver hair. I thought about pulling out a five and throwing it at him, but remembered I didn't have my wallet. Then it hit me how sharply and well-dressed he was—obviously not needy. His sweater sleeves were pushed up on his forearms revealing a long since faded military tattoo of a shield with two swords crossing over the front of it, indicating that he'd possibly been a tough character once. I turned my head toward the lake waiting for him to go about his way, but after thirty seconds or so I could sense he was still standing there, watching me. Thirty seconds is a long time when you are counting the seconds.

"You don't give up easily do you?" I said, jerking my head back around in disbelief, feeling the buzz from my Red Bull. "You're a stubborn old guy!"

"Too old to give up," he said. "Learned that sometimes you gotta stand your ground and fight for what's important."

"Well good for you. Me, I'm tired of fighting. Besides I don't have any money on me anyway."

"Don't want your money," he replied. "Just want to paint your portrait. My painting is a gift."

"A gift?" I let out a sarcastic laugh. "Are you for real, man?"

"Pretty sure I am," he chuckled, feeling his arms and legs.

"Look," I said, standing up from the bench to bolt. "I'm dealing with some serious stuff right now—very serious. I don't have time for this. If you're not leaving, I am."

His back stiffened and instead of retreating, he actually moved a step closer, now almost in my face like a drill sergeant, or a coach. Shocked at this, my first inclination was to shove him away and run, but for some peculiar reason I did just the opposite. I froze. His eyes narrowed and brows furrowed. "Sit down!" he thundered with an absolute authority that seemed to originate from far beyond him. "You must stop your running! You *need* your portrait painted!"

Dazed, I staggered backward and dropped down on the bench. What was going on here? What was I doing? He was just some old eccentric painter who was probably off in the head. He had no authority over me. Yet if that was the case, why did it feel like he did? At that precise moment the sun burst through the clouds casting down rays that illuminated his face. As the beams of light shone on him, his countenance softened and his eyes called out, pleading, reaching beyond my coldness and cynicism, penetrating to my core causing my pent-up anger to fade and a calmness to rest upon me. As I gave in to this soothing sensation, he sat down on the bench next to me and I scooted over offering him more room. Squinting, he shielded the light from his eyes with one hand and pointed out over the lake with the other. "See those ducks over there?"

I followed his finger to a particular group of smaller ducks flocked around some reeds. "Yes," I said curiously.

"Those are Hooded Mergansers," he explained. "Did you know they're one of the few breeds of duck that actually migrate north to spend winters? Something special. Don't see them much. They're one of North America's most magnificent but rarest mallards. You know why they call them Hooded Mergansers?"

"No sir."

"They have a sail-shaped white crown on their heads that can expand or collapse. It makes their head look oversized, like they're wearing a big ole hood. Quite fascinating. But most people don't even notice. Just pass right on by. ...And when the sunlight reflects off their feathers it makes their colors blaze." A gust of wind swirled up the leaves around us.

He patted my leg and unfolded his long frame to stand up. "Sometimes people don't realize the special things that are right there under their noses."

I let out a deep sigh. "All right," I said throwing my hands up. "How long's this gonna take?"

The old man's eyes locked back onto mine with a kind-hearted stare that pierced right through me. "Now, that depends on you," he said with not so much as a blink. "That all depends on you."

4

The old gentleman calmly walked the twenty or so feet and retrieved his cart from the trail. He then positioned it directly in front of where I was sitting and began preparing his work. Sitting there without my iPhone on me, I started to get fidgety. Time was passing and I needed to check my messages. Because of a major deadline the pressure was on at work. This was the first Saturday I'd had off in over a month, but I was still on call. I'd be okay for a while if there wasn't a crisis.

Really, I wanted to text Paige and Josh. Now that the insanity was lifting, I needed to check on her and let her know how bad and stupid I felt. I figured it couldn't hurt, though I also figured it wouldn't do much good either. It's frightening how anger can blind me and how differently I feel after stepping back from the situation and cooling down a bit. Hopefully Paige felt the same way and we could make up.

Surely this portrait thing wouldn't take that long—twenty, thirty minutes tops. As much as I wanted to get away, there was something about this guy that kept me glued to the bench. For some reason I felt safe with him, like I'd known him forever. Besides, I needed to be somewhere other than home right now. If I just went with it, I'd be back soon enough. What could it hurt?

"Okay," I said taking a deep breath, still not believing I was actually taking part in such an eccentric activity. "Paint me. The clock is ticking."

The old gentleman glanced up at me then dropped his head back down and continued sorting through his supplies, apparently unfazed by my comments. "It's important for an artist to think before he works," he said. "I'm thinking how to paint you, in order to catch your soul. You see, oil reflects a completely different likeness than watercolor or sketch." Scratching his chin, not the least bit uncomfortable or threatened, he went on. "You know what I think?"

"I'm afraid to ask."

"I think watercolor fits you. Watercolor dribbles and makes splotches. It's not neat and clean—doesn't stay in the boundaries—gives a more impressionistic look. And watercolor is vulnerable to its surroundings. You know, the temperature and breezes, even the angle of the paper. A watercolor work reflects every bit of contact the painter makes. Each stroke of the brush leaves an imprint just like each experience in this ole life leaves an imprint on us and others. You can't hide or cover up anything in watercolor. You have to blend in your mistakes to create a unique work. Mistakes become part of its character—makes it special. You can't undo them, so you use them to make the work stronger."

"Great," I smirked. "With all my mistakes this should be a Van Gogh!"

With that, he smiled and pulled out a thick piece of watercolor paper from a cylinder, gently unrolled it, smoothed it out with his hands and then fastened it to the easel with some clips. The easel adjusted and he brought it to a slight angle, almost flat like a table, but not quite. Then he unfolded a portable stool and sat.

"Did you know that you are made up of seventy percent water?" he continued. "Your blood is eighty-three percent water, lungs eighty, brain eighty-five, and your muscles seventy-five. Sounds impossible, but it's true."

"I took biology."

"Then you know that water is necessary for your body to digest and absorb vitamins and nutrients. It detoxifies the liver and kidneys and carries waste away from the body. When you're dehydrated your blood becomes thicker because of the lack of water, and your body has to work that much harder to cause the blood to circulate. As a result, your body feels fatigued. We need water for our survival. You're dehydrated in spirit—struggling hard to survive in this life—working hard, but seeing limited results. So...I think I'll paint you with water."

"Is it *that* obvious?" I asked.

He raised one eyebrow and smiled.

"You take this painting stuff pretty seriously don't you," I said. "You sure you don't want any money, because I told you I forgot my wallet?"

"Like I said, painting's my gift and a gift is only a gift if it is received. If you pay for it, then it's not a gift, now is it?"

"How come I get the feeling you are doing more than painting a picture here?"

"Just exercising my gift."

I exhaled a long breath of air. "I'm going to be here awhile, aren't I?"

"Need to use my cell?"

"Uh...yes," I stuttered, "as a matter of fact, I do."

After handing me his slightly outdated Blackberry, I started texting while he took out the plastic jug of water and poured some into a glass jar.

"Paige," I texted, taking great care to cover the screen so the old guy couldn't see. "Look." Suddenly I was unsure of what to say. "I should not have said—" Pausing a second, I pushed Delete and started typing again. "Paige I—" Backspace. Backspace. "Paige—" Delete. I finally typed, "Paige, I love you." and pushed Send. Then I entered Josh's text. "Josh, Mom told me what happened. We need to talk. It's important. I'll be home soon. Don't disappear on me!"

I handed the phone back to the old painter, who was now dipping his brush from the jar of water onto the well-used palette in his hands. After a couple of dips and swirls in the paint, he started to touch the paper, but then quickly drew back his arm.

"Now just go on and look at me," he said. "Here I am about to paint your portrait and I haven't even introduced myself." He set the brush down and extended his right hand. "Name is James Edward Porter. Friends call me Jim Ed. Nice to meet you."

His grip was firm and confident, yet trembled ever so slightly. "My name is Adam Camp. It's nice to meet you Jim Ed. Look, I'm sorry I've been kind of a jerk today."

He let out a hearty laugh. "We're all jerks sometimes, Adam."

Noting the lack of criticism, I asked, "What's up with the Saints hat?"

"Oh, I grew up down that way," said Jim Ed, "Couple of my relatives were hit pretty hard by Katrina a few years back and we opened up our home to them for a while. They brought me the hat." He lifted it off his head and looked at it. "It's special. You know the Saints won the Super Bowl in 09."

"Yep," I said. "Don't remind me. They beat my Vikings in the NFC Championship Game!"

Jim Ed placed the white hat back on his silver-haired head. The easel stood about five or six feet away and because of its slight angle I could not see his creation. That didn't matter though, for I was focused totally on the colorful expressions illuminating Jim Ed's face and his hands gliding the brush up and down and around on the paper as if he were directing a grand symphony. Clearly, to him this was much more than a portrait; it was an expression of his very soul.

5

"Is it all right if I talk some?" I asked feeling fidgety again. "Or would that mess you up? I can get a little chatty when I'm nervous."

"Talking's fine by me," said Jim Ed completing a stroke with a slight slap of his brush against the paper. "But why in the world would you be nervous? I'm just an old painter."

"Maybe nervous wasn't the best word choice," I said. "It's more like anxious. I've got a lot on my mind and getting my portrait painted at the park today was *not* something on my 'to do' list." I gave him a tight smile.

"Some of the best things in life are unplanned," he said never missing a beat. "Got to live in the moment."

"You gotta admit though, it's a little strange."

Jim Ed blinked innocently. "I guess it is a bit, as you kids like to say, 'out of the box.' But trust me, Adam. Living 'inside the box' will eventually suffocate a person. I've got to have an outlet of expression."

"Okay, I get painting, but why stalk down strangers? For all I know you could have had a gun or something. Aren't you worried about how people may perceive you? Why not just paint one of those Hooded Mergansers?"

Jim Ed paused a moment considering my questions. His pause made me regret asking, for he wasn't breaking any speed records for painting. When he talked, his brush slowed almost to a stop. "Can't let what others think stop me from doing what I'm supposed to be doing," he said. "My painting's not about me. I told you it's a gift." Jim Ed scratched his forehead with the wooden tip of the brush and glanced out over the lake. A crisp breeze raked leaves across the ground and our feet again. "And I'll tell you something else," he continued. "When I'm exercising my gift, I'm filled with peace. You know that feeling you get when you're doing something and while you're doing it calmness just takes you over, like you're feeling God's pleasure? I feel it right now. Can't explain it very well, but I know that I'm doing right, that I am right where I'm supposed to be. When I paint and do what I do, well, I guess I feel like one of those ducks in the water over there. They don't know why they need to be in it, they just know they're supposed to be, and they're at ease when they are."

"How come I haven't seen you around here before?"

"Oh, I'm around. The world's a big place. Don't always paint people though, only when I feel directed to them."

"You felt directed to me?"

"Yes, sir. Sure did. Really it was more like 'sent.'"

"Sent? Oh yeah? Who sent ya?"

"God."

Crap. My stomach clenched and those angry, anxious feelings burst right back to the surface. I punched myself in the thigh with my fist for being such a sucker. *I knew it! This guy's looney! Suffering from dementia or something. Escaped from a home. They're probably looking for him right now!* I jumped to my feet and made a move toward the trail. "That's it," I shouted over my shoulder. "I've got to go! See ya later, man!"

Jim Ed dropped his brush and jerked his body upright. "Adam!" he thundered once again, this time louder with even more authority than before. "Look at me!"

I kept on walking. "I go to church, man!" I blasted. "I've heard enough preaching to last me three lifetimes! I don't have time for this nonsense!"

"You think this is about church?" Jim Ed shouted. "This is about saving your marriage and your son! It's about saving your life! Becoming the man you were created to be!"

For the second time that day, I stopped dead in my tracks. "My marriage?" I whispered to myself. "My son? …How'd he know?" I had covered the screen carefully. There's no way he saw anything. Fear of losing my family gripped me. My legs wobbled and tears began to pressure the back of my eyes. "Who are you?" I asked, now facing him. "What is this?"

An inviting warmness bathed Jim Ed's face. "Just let me finish the painting," he said with empathy in his voice, peace exuding from his very essence. "This is right where you need to be."

6

We sat in silence for some time as Jim Ed poured himself into his masterpiece. Some children were playing soccer in an open field across the trail. While mindlessly watching them run back and forth, I replayed my argument with Paige. *"It wasn't supposed to be like this! I can't take this anymore! Something's got to change Adam."*

"Change! ...Oh, you mean me, right? I've got to change?"

Pain jabbed my gut. *"I've had enough. I want out. I've got to get out."* Surely she couldn't mean it? After all these years? After all we'd been through? My heart rate became rapid. Panic seized me again and I panted for breath.

"You idiot," the voice in my head was back, assaulting, accusing, mocking. *"You blew it. It's over. Paige doesn't care enough about you to even stay and fight. Why should she? You're a loser. Who'd want to fight for you? She's gonna have men lining up. Wait and see. Someone who can give her a real life. And don't forget your boy. He's so ending up in jail. Rehab time! It's gonna cost you big too. He's flushing his future down the toilet. Maybe he'll move in with his mother? Well, at least you have your work. That's what you're married to anyway."* With a clenched jaw, I ground my teeth. My dentist was going to have a heyday. *"And what are you doing wasting time sitting here with this old clown? He's crazy you know."*

"Shut...up," I ordered under my breath.

Never looking up, Jim Ed dabbed his brush in the glass of water, touched it on the palette, and then brought it back to the paper. It was as if he'd been waiting, calculating how long to let me wrestle with my thoughts. "Want to talk about it?" he finally probed.

I turned my gaze from the kids playing soccer to Jim Ed. Unlike with Eric, I felt I could let my guard down. "It's been a pretty rough day," I sighed, "year really." My eyes wandered to the lake's edge where the Hooded Mergansers were splashing around doing what ducks do. Smaller than regular ducks, their shimmering black wings had long white stripes running from neck to tail and the males had black heads crowned with white crests and flaming orange eyes. Jim Ed said it looked like they were wearing hoods. I thought it looked more like Mohawks. Exquisitely and flawlessly designed, the Hooded Mergansers glided through the water with grace and ease like they understood they were exactly where they were supposed to be, doing exactly what they were created to do. What was I created to do?

"You're right," I said. "They are remarkable creatures. I've been to this park dozens of times and never even gave them a second glance. I tell you what though—" I paused to consider whether to continue.

Jim Ed placed his brush down again so he could fully absorb my words. "Go ahead," he encouraged.

I ran my hand through my hair nervously. "All right," I said. "But this is weird. I've never talked to anyone like this. Not even my own father, not that he would have been interested."

"Sometimes it's easier to open up to an outsider." At that moment a ding came up on Jim Ed's Blackberry indicating a message. "Excuse me a sec," he said twisting his body around to pick up his cell from his cart. After reviewing the message he held it out toward me. "Here, it's for you."

I grabbed it and read the text.

"Who is this!?" Paige had sent. Then it occurred to me that I had not identified myself in my text and Paige had never seen Jim Ed's number. Again, I felt stupid. That was par for the course.

"Paige, this is Adam," I typed back. "I left my cell at home so I used a friend's. I needed to tell you how bad I feel. I didn't mean it. Maybe we could go out to dinner tonight?" I knew it was a long shot, but I was grasping at straws. I pushed Send and held the phone in my hand, waiting while Jim Ed continued painting. After a while it was obvious Paige wasn't going to reply, so I handed it back to him.

He took the phone out of my hand with a sympathetic look and placed it back in the cart. "You were saying?"

A huge white goose wobbled up to the bench honking. It was loud and annoying. "Get!" I shouted, shooing it with my hands. "Get out of here!" It stuck its long neck and beak in the air as if saying, "Well, I never!" and then wandered off.

"Adam, you were saying?"

My head dropped. "I don't know now."

"It's okay. I'm safe."

I locked my hands behind my head and leaned back. "I was about to say that I don't feel at peace like you or those ducks out there. I certainly don't feel God's pleasure, if such a thing even exists."

"Trust me, it exists," said Jim Ed.

"I tell you what I do feel. I feel stress! Yeah, that's what I feel, stress…and anger…and guilt…and disappointment. I could go on and on. You got a notebook and pen on you? I'll fill it up!" An emotional dam was breaking inside me and all this stuff was spilling out. "I'm drained, dried up, and burnt out…and I'm unhappy, Jim Ed! I can't remember the last time I actually enjoyed life. I deal with pressures all day long and demanding clients. I'm on the road way too much. If I see another airport I'm going to croak! When I finally get home I'm worn out and on edge. But here's the funny thing; Paige and my communication is actually better when I'm away!

"Now she's thinking about leaving me. May have already left. And our son's an addict. We're watching him flush his future down the toilet! I don't know what to do. I didn't sign up for this! How'd my life turn out like this? I'm ashamed to say this, but there have been days when I feel so beat up I've considered ending it all. This very morning, right when you walked up, I was fantasizing about leaving everything—just walking away or maybe going to sleep and never waking up. There's no contentment in my life, none. And peace? I don't even know what that means at this point. I'm numb Jim Ed, just plain numb."

Jim Ed chewed on my words carefully before finally responding. "Numbness can be the greatest predator," he said. "You're in a war whether you realize it or not. Denying it or going numb as you say causes you to lose your passion for life. God gave you emotions for a reason. Sometimes you got to get scared enough or angry enough to fight. Filling your life with substitutes just anesthetizes the hole inside you.

It's the enemy's way of keeping you disengaged and keeping you from fighting for what's important."

"I told you I'm tired of fighting," I said. "It seems the more I fight, the worse things get. It's like I'm in quicksand. The more I struggle to get ahead, the further behind I get. I'm done fighting. Paige doesn't understand."

Jim Ed got very still, thinking. A group of college-age girls power walked by, laughing and talking loudly. He let them pass before he opened his mouth. "Sounds to me like you've got to get yourself a new pair of eyes," he said. "Change the way you're seeing."

"Huh?" I said, tilting my head confused. "I can see just fine, dude. My life pretty much sucks right now. That's crystal clear."

Jim Ed leaned forward to emphasize his point. "You know Adam, great artists have great vision. They have the ability to see beyond the surface deep into the soul of what they are painting. The difference between an average work and a masterpiece is a masterpiece doesn't copy. It captures. Captures the soul of the subject and then reflects that soul onto the canvas."

"What's that got to do with me?" I asked. "I'm no artist, that's for sure. Couldn't paint my way out of a wet paper bag."

"People paint all kinds of portraits, Adam," Jim Ed continued, "just not always with a brush. Their life is a canvas, and they are the brush. Like this brush in my hand leaves an impression with each stroke, they leave an impression on everything they do or come in contact with. And one day, when they're stretched out in their coffin, there'll be a portrait of their life that somebody's going to be looking over. What kind of portrait is your life painting, Adam Camp?"

The question hit me unexpectedly like a two-by-four right between the eyes. My whole body stiffened. *What kind of portrait is my life painting?* Part of me was offended. I mean the nerve of asking such a question. *"Adam Camp, what kind of portrait is your life painting?"* As Jim Ed went back to work and I watched him dancing with the brush in his hands, the truth about me began to sink in. My shoulders sank because I was all too aware of what kind of impressions I'd been leaving—ruts, debris, rubble, wreckage. The fact was, if I had died on that day, the picture of my life would look more like graffiti scribbled on a wall with a few expletives rather than a beautiful portrait.

"You're not making me feel any better," I said.

"Not trying to make you feel better," he said. "Trying to get you refocused. To paint a life masterpiece you first have to develop the eyes of an artist and learn to really see the things around you, into their soul, feel their pain."

Shifting in my seat, I tugged at my sweatshirt. "What about saving my marriage and family? I thought we were going to talk about that?"

"Changing your marriage and family starts with changing you."

My eyebrows lifted. "Did you talk to Paige?"

"No. Why?"

"Never mind."

"And the first step to changing you is changing your vision. To do that, you need a little eye surgery."

"Does it hurt?" I asked.

"It gets worse before it gets better."

Jim Ed lifted his hat and wiped his brow with his forearm. "I need you to try and keep your head up if you can," he said while dipping his brush in the color-smeared pallet again then making a swirl on the paper. He looked up toward me, scratching his chin, contemplating. "When I'm looking at you in order to capture your soul, you know what I'm trying to see?"

I shrugged my shoulders.

"I'm not focusing on your outside. I'm trying to find the masterpiece inside you."

"Good luck with that," I said, knowing all too well what was inside me.

"You know who Michelangelo is?"

"Yes, he painted the Sistine Chapel, right?"

"Michelangelo was perhaps the greatest artist of the Renaissance period—a painter and a sculptor. Yes he painted some divine masterpieces, but he also worked chisel and stone. When asked where he drew the inspiration for his famous 'David' sculpture that stands in Florence, you know what Michelangelo said?"

"You got me."

"He said when he first looked at that rough block of stone he knew David was imprisoned somewhere inside, and it was his divine calling as an artist to find him and set him free.

So he began chipping away everything that wasn't David. Michelangelo had eyes that saw past the surface into the soul. He saw that uneven, irregular, and imperfect stone... and that's how God sees you, Adam. The first step in changing your vision is changing how you see yourself. There's a David inside you, Adam, a mighty warrior. We've got to find him and set him free."

"I'm no David," I said. "You need to talk to Eric." I let out a cynical laugh. "He thinks he's David and Samson combined."

"Who?"

"Just some guy I know from church—perfect marriage, perfect kids, perfect life."

"That you know of," said Jim Ed. "Trust me. He's got issues too. Besides, David had plenty of issues in his life. He made a ton of mistakes and even committed some hideous sins. David wasn't everyone's hero by a long shot. Yet he was still a great warrior and a man after God's own heart."

"Whatever," I said, releasing another long breath of discouragement.

"Hang with me, Adam. I think you'll be glad you did."

"Keep going," I said.

"There were times when it seemed the whole world was against David," he said. "The people closest to him abandoned him. They misunderstood him. I mean at one point, they wanted to string him up. And David had a heap of family problems—wives and kids who disrespected him. David brought a lot of it on himself too. He wasn't known for his great fathering abilities. But in all of it, you know what David did?"

"No."

"He encouraged himself in the Lord."

"What does that mean?"

"At first glance it sounds simple, but when you break it down, it's profound. In essence, it means David knew who he was and understood the source of his strength. He understood his real identity regardless what others thought of him or how rotten his life seemed. He understood his identity and his enemy. Even in the deepest pits of despair and failure, David was secure in who he was, or should I say who his God was. Listen to this."

Jim Ed stopped painting and reached into his cart. He fumbled around, pulling out an old, faded leather Bible, its pages tattered and edges rolled up. After opening it, he slowly flipped through the pages, stopped, and began to read. *"Lord, how they have increased who trouble me! Many are they who rise up against me. Many are they who say of me, 'There is no help for him in God.'* In other words, 'David, you're so messed up even God's abandoned you!' But hear David's response in that same passage. *'But You O, Lord, are a shield for me, My glory and the One who lifts my head.'* His security wasn't in anyone but God. Now that gets me excited! At times David had to stand his ground alone, but eventually the same people who doubted him, who even betrayed him, rallied around him."

Jim Ed closed the Bible and his eyes narrowed. "Adam, your insecurity is killing you and it's driving Paige away. She can't respect someone who doesn't respect himself."

I bristled at the comment, but deep down I knew he was right.

"You know what I think?" he continued, picking up his brush and dabbing at something on the paper.

"Surprise me," I said, cracking my neck. It was a nervous habit.

"I think you'd rather live alone and unloved than to be in a relationship filled with disrespect."

"When I'm alone there's less stress," I admitted, "Less hassle."

"You mean less conflict?"

"Yes, you nailed it!" I said, "Except the conflict with myself! I pretty much despise myself!"

"Well that's something that needs addressing, don't you think?" He leaned forward, brush still flowing on the paper, and spoke softly. "Starts with refocusing your view. Get you seeing yourself as God sees you."

"The way God sees me?" I laughed again. "I can tell you how God sees me, as a failure, a big fat zero!"

Jim Ed stopped the flow of his brush and looked at me long and hard. "When you see God's love for you, you can begin to see yourself more clearly, the way your Creator, the Master Artist, sees you. That's where your true identity and purpose comes from. Takes some adjustment and usually occurs in the middle of pain, but it'll free you to live."

I said nothing, nor did I move.

8

Jim Ed studied my profile and then studied the paper like a master chess player would calculate his next move. "You know I do understand what it's like to despise yourself." He removed his glasses and rubbed his nose with his thumb and index finger while still holding the brush. "I know all about hating oneself."

The comment caused me to jolt upright on the bench. "I find that hard to believe," I said. "You seem so happy and at peace."

"Happy is a relative term," he said, "but I am at peace... now. I had to learn, like you have to learn, to see myself as the Master Artist sees me." He placed his bifocals back on and adjusted them on his nose. "You can't even imagine what it was like growing up as a black man in the South back then. Things are a lot different now."

I didn't see that coming either. It was hard to imagine how this intelligent, respectful, compassionate man could have been subject to ignorance and prejudice. Jim Ed's eyes got a faraway look and made me wonder what long ago memory he was seeing.

Mama Porter placed the shiny bright dime in little Jim Ed's hand and squeezed it shut. "I be real proud of you, son. You worked yourself hard this week—helped your Mama out so good. Now go on and pick whatever candy you want. You deserve it."

Little Jim Ed stared down at his hand, slowly unfolding his fingers, hardly believing his eyes. Ten whole cents! His mind danced with the possibilities as he tiptoed to get a clearer view of the myriad of candies behind the glass counter in Simmons Corner Store. There were jars of jelly beans, licorice sticks, both red and black, candy corn, Life Savers, homemade cookies, and a huge jar of dill pickles. After quite a while deliberating with himself, Jim Ed finally came to a decision.

"I'll takes me some jelly beans," he said, "and some candy corn...and...and...one of them pickles."

Harry Simmons, a gentle and caring man wearing a white apron, scooped up a heap of jelly beans and candy corn pieces and poured them into a small brown bag. Then he fished around the pickle jar in an attempt to snag the largest one possible and put it into separate brown bag.

"Now what you say to Mr. Simmons?" Mama Porter asked Jim Ed as Mr. Simmons bent down and handed him the bags.

"Ahh, thank you, Mr. Simmons."

Jim Ed was thoroughly enjoying his pickle while at the same time firmly gripping his bag of candy when he and his mama stepped through the front door of the store to exit. That also happened to be the exact moment when a young girl came running pell-mell into the store, plowing squarely into Jim Ed. The collision knocked him to the floor, sending the pickle and jelly beans mixed with candy corn flying. Determined not to lose a single piece, little Jim Ed scrambled around on the store's hardwood floor in a desperate effort to retrieve them. While doing so, the girl's mom said to her, in a well-mannered voice, yet loud enough that everybody in the store could hear, "Now Elizabeth, you say 'excuse me' to the little colored boy."

"Mommmm," the girl protested in her frilly dress, "do I have to? He's a nigger."

"Yes you do," the mother insisted, with a slightly embarrassed look on her face, "and what have I told you about using that word? He can't help it that he's colored."

"But Mommmm, you and Daddy say it all the time!"

The woman and her daughter's words seared through Jim Ed's heart like red-hot daggers. Mama Porter wanted to get in the mother's face and tell her a word or two, but doing so would only mean more trouble for her and her family. So she gritted her teeth and bore it.

Picking up the now dirty pieces of candy and placing them back into his bag, Jim Ed was ever so careful to exclude each and every black jelly bean. Holding the rejects tightly, he walked back up to the counter and held out his hand toward Mr. Simmons.

"Please take these black ones back. I don't want them."

Mr. Simmons smiled back empathetically while taking the black ones out of the boy's hand. Then he scooped up some new jelly beans, sorted out the black ones and picked him out another pickle. Mama Porter nodded to Mr. Simmons indicating her appreciation for his kindness toward her son.

The next stop Mama Porter had was to run into Woolworth's to pick up some fabric for sewing.

"Mama, that pickle made me thirsty," Jim Ed said, tugging at his mother's dress. "Can I gets me a drink of water?"

"Sure honey," Mama Porter said, unrolling a piece of fabric and examining it. "There's a water fountain right by the bathrooms, next to the toys. Juss go all the way downs that aisle right

there," she pointed, "and you'll sees it. I'll be here waiting whens you finish. I has to pick out some more cloth."

At that, Jim Ed meandered his way through the toy section, stopping of course, to check out a new yo-yo and a cap-gun/holster set with a matching cowboy hat, but the thirst got the best of him and he eventually made it to the opposite end of the store. When he bent over to take a gulp of water from the brand-new, shiny clean, water fountain—one with a cooler to keep the water nice and cold, some older kids surrounded him yelling, "Hey nigger boy, you caint drink there. Caint you read? Says 'Whites Only.'" Jerking Jim Ed back by the collar they ordered, "You gotta drink from your own fountain over there!" Then they pointed to a door that opened up to the back of the store's alley. Outside was a filthy, smelly, rusty old water faucet next to an equally filthy bathroom door. While Jim Ed went outside for his drink, the boys guarded the "White's Only" fountain making sure he obeyed the law. What little water did come out of the old faucet was hot and tasted like its smell...nasty. When Jim Ed finally made it back to his mother, tears were streaming down his cheeks.

"What's wrong, my angel?" Mama Porter asked.

Jim Ed wiped his eyes and looked up at his mother. "Mama, why are people so mean to us because we colored?"

"It ain't right, honey, but it be the way things is," she said. "It be the way things is."

"I tell you, Adam, I despised myself for being black—despised the color black. The road we walked on was black.

Black was the color of dirt and storm clouds. I always felt like I had some infectious disease or something. I was angry at God for making me that way. After a while, being called a 'nigger' for so long and being treated that way, I guess I just started believing it—didn't think I was worth the dirt in my own Mama's front yard."

"I'm really sorry you experienced that," I said, cringing inside. "Prejudice is an ugly thing."

"Yeah, it's ugly all right. You wouldn't believe some of the terrible, ignorant things I've seen people do in my lifetime. But just the same, I've learned over the years that you can't thrive in life while blaming all your problems on others. You'll always wind up a victim. Besides, things are better nowadays. We've come a long way and so have you, although we have a long way to go—still a lot of healing to do."

"I hope so," I said, thinking of my father and grandfather and some of my relatives, how they lived in a cesspool of discrimination and bigotry. I wondered how I would have acted if I'd been raised back then, in that setting. It was not something I enjoyed thinking about, but ignoring it seemed worse.

"So what happened?" I asked. "Where'd all the hate and anger go? Why are you painting this white guy's portrait?"

"Well, *my* change didn't happen all at once, but little by little, starting when I met Christina—my dearest Christina." Jim Ed's face lit up. "I tell you, Adam, we have to always be alert because God sends significant people into our lives at critical moments. Christina came to me during one of mine."

9

"Christina?" I said, a slight smile fighting to form on my face. "Is this a love story, Jim Ed?"

"Yes-sir-ree," he replied, "could be a movie on the Hallmark Channel." He lowered his head a few inches from the paper and blew air on a spot he'd just painted. "Christina, well she…how can I put it? She was the most beautiful woman ever laid my eyes on—walked with grace and dignity—always held her head up high, even in the midst of our struggles. Was humble, understanding how much she needed God's mercy and grace in her life, but at the same time had this glowing confidence about her."

"Sounds like a special lady," I said, trying to create an image of Christina in my mind.

"Oh, she was special indeed. It was just like the song says, 'she was a magnet and I was steel.' Something about her just drew me to her. I'd been around lots of pretty girls in my day. I may not be much to look at now, but back then," Jim Ed chuckled, "I was considered quite a catch…but none of those other girls could hold a light to my Christina. She's the one who helped me see that I was special. Made me a better man.

"I'd be getting all down on myself or fighting mad for being who I was and she'd tell me things like, 'Jim Ed, did you know that black is the color of the richest most fertile soil? Black soil is the best.' I remember we were walking by Mr. Hatcher's field one day and she said to me, 'You see that shiny black steed over there? Your color is the same as it. Isn't it a spectacular creature—strong and confident?' She'd place her hands on my cheeks and pull my face down to hers and say, 'Now you listen to me, James Edward Porter, you are created in God's image. You hear me?' I guess after a while, I started to believe that too.

"Let me show you something." With his palette still in one hand and his brush in the other, Jim Ed walked over to me. "Here, hold out your arm."

I stretched out my arm toward him as he began to dip the brush in the paint. He gently brushed a stroke of yellow on my arm, then red, then blue, then green.

"What do those colors make up?" he asked.

"A rainbow?" I guessed.

"Yep, a rainbow."

After that, he repeated the process on my other arm. This time however, he painted each stroke directly on top of each other.

"Now what color you have?"

"Black."

"That's right," he said grinning large and wide. "Black is all the colors of the rainbow put together."

"That's pretty neat, Jim Ed," I said. We'd only been talking for a short while and somehow this stranger had already touched me in an overwhelming way. "Christina showed me that one day. Taught me how to receive love and respect myself for who I was, to see myself as God sees me. I had to get new eyes, Adam, like you. When we begin to see ourselves the way God sees us, something miraculous begins to happen. We start seeing others the way God sees them and loving them the way God loves us. When that happens, people start seeing us differently. "

I nodded, indicating I was following him.

"You want Paige to see you differently? Then start seeing yourself as God sees you and seeing her how God sees her. It's an unending circle."

"Sounds too simple," I said, giving him my skeptical look. I wanted desperately to believe what he was saying, but because I'd been so beat down with the Bible and religion all my life, I was a bit leery. I'd heard the "God loves me" spiel, but deep down I'd also felt He was angry at me and most certainly didn't like me, especially given the fact that I'd failed Him so much. On top of that, I could be a real jerk, like Paige had so poignantly pointed out.

"Is simple," said Jim Ed. He could see that I was struggling. "So simple, people miss it. But it's not simplistic. There is a difference you know. Many profound things are simple, can be understood by a child but still baffle a scholar. Man's pride gets in the way. Want things to be complicated, but you're right. It is simple."

He got quiet, shifted his gaze from me back to the portrait. I could see the faint gleam of sweat on his shiny forehead as he worked. The crisp morning was turning into a quite warm day. My stomach growled and I closed my eyes.

"And sing," Jim Ed suddenly spoke making my eyes pop right back open. "My Christina could sing like an angel. Her favorite song was 'Amazing Grace.' I can hear her singing it right now in front of the church, the whole congregation swaying like a wheat field in the wind. 'Amazzzzing grace, how sweet the sound…that saved a *wretch* like meeeee!' She'd be singing and then stop right in the middle and start preaching. She'd say, 'If you took the word *wretch* out of this song, it'd change the whole meaning.' Think about that, Adam."

I didn't respond with words, just let my head drop and clasped my hands together in my lap thinking about what he'd just said.

"Her daddy was the preacher at Mount Zion Church, but Christina, she wasn't just a churchgoer, that girl knew God. There's a big difference. A lot of church folk out there. Few people have a direct line to the Throne like her. She used to tell me that I was priceless because God created me and loved me so much that He died for me, took every bit of my sin on that Cross. He paid the price completely. She'd say, 'Why you so mad Jim Ed? God's not mad at you. All His anger was taken out on Jesus. Thank God for the blood! Now you receive His gift! Don't be trying to atone for your sins. You can't do it. It's already done! He was the propitiation.' She loved that word, propitiation. 'But you gotta believe it, that He's offering it to you, that if you were the only person alive, God would have still sent Jesus to the Cross to pay the price for you. When you hate yourself for being black, it's like saying God makes junk and my God don't make junk! Don't be calling God a liar!' Jim Ed paused, took a breath. "It's simple but not easy, you know."

"What's not that easy?" I asked.

"Accepting God's gift," he replied. "I mean really believing it and receiving it. We either think we are too good and don't need it, or too bad and don't deserve it. Especially when we see ourselves like we really are. Truth is; we're all wretches. We all fall short of God's glory and are in need of redemption."

"I'm hearing you," I said. "But whatever happened to Christina?"

"I married her almost sixty years ago."

"That's what I figured," I said, shifting in my seat to get comfortable. "Sixty years, wow, that's quite an accomplishment."

"It sure is, especially in today's world. We live in a society today that is set against marriage and the enemy is out to destroy it. The two are working hand in hand."

"Okay, so how'd you two meet? You can't stop now."

"Well, it's quite a story. I'll tell you what. How 'bout we trade stories—you meeting Paige for my meeting Christina?"

I paused for a moment considering his request. "No thanks," I finally said. "I'd rather just listen to yours right now if you don't mind."

"Don't mind at all," said Jim Ed. At that moment, he turned to his paper and began rubbing furiously at a spot with a rag before he daubed first one color then the other. "Your face changed completely when you were thinking about Paige," he said in a matter-of-fact voice, again, not even looking up from his fingers.

"Really?"

"Yep," he said. "It softened." Jim Ed laid down the brush and studied his progress with a satisfied expression, then continued his own story.

10

"It was in nineteen hundred fifty-four," Jim Ed said looking up to the sky in another effort to recall the past. "And—" His Blackberry dinged again and he paused to pick it up. "Here, it's for you," he said. "Looks like it's from Paige again."

I took the phone in my hand and silently read her text. "What friend? Words mean nothing to me anymore, Adam. I've lost trust." I stared down at the phone and reread it, her words ripping my guts out. I didn't even respond.

"You look like you just bit into a rotten apple and found yourself a worm," said Jim Ed.

"Oh, I found a worm all right—me," I said. As I uttered those words, a wave of self-loathing pounded me. "I totally blew it with her this morning. We had an argument and I cut her up pretty bad. It seems cutting people up is one of my gifts."

Jim Ed nodded his head indicating he was listening while never stopping the flow of painting.

"Actually, we cut each other up," I continued. "She's pretty gifted too. Said she was sorry she married me...that she wants out."

"Do you believe her?"

"Truthfully, Jim Ed, I don't know what to believe." I sighed deeply for about the tenth time that morning. "We've been drifting apart for a while now, but have been too busy to deal with it. We just go about our business, ignoring the elephant in the room. Now, suddenly, it's like all hell is breaking loose and we're being ripped apart at the seams. The situation with Josh isn't helping matters either."

"That tends to happen when we let things build up over time—don't deal with issues when they are just small, like pebbles in a stream. You keep piling them up one by one and eventually the flow of water is cut off."

"Paige and I used to be best friends, Jim Ed. I mean best friends. We did everything together. These days it's more like we're two irritated roommates, invading each other's space, stepping on one another's toes. She's annoyed with me all the time, and she's built these walls around herself, determined to keep me out. She checks out on me. Drives me crazy! It's like I'm talking to a blank wall most of the time. She never listens to me or opens up anymore."

"Why would she?" he said. "I wouldn't."

"Pardon me?" I asked, again startled by Jim Ed's bluntness.

"Maybe her checking out is a way of protecting herself? I mean, why would she open up to you if everything you've been saying about yourself is true? How can she trust someone who's cheated on her time and time again?"

"Now wait just a doggone minute! We may not have the happiest marriage right now, but I have never cheated on her! Never!"

"You sure about that?"

"Of course I'm sure! I think that's something I'd remember. Look, I may not like myself, but I love my wife!"

"Did you know, Adam, there are adulteries of the heart? She trusted you emotionally, and you dishonored that trust.

She gave you her heart and needed to feel significant, but instead felt betrayed. Your wife has put up walls and doesn't open up to you anymore because you have crushed her spirit. After being wounded time and time again, she doesn't feel safe around you any longer. Nobody in their right mind will continue to allow themselves to be hurt over and over again like that. It's only natural that she would put up walls."

"You talk like everything's my fault," I declared. "She's got issues too! She can be vicious!"

"You ever saw a caged possum?" asked Jim Ed.

"What?"

"Have you ever seen a caged possum?"

"Only in the movies," I replied with an edge.

"They're sweet little things until they're backed into a corner and feel threatened." Jim Ed formed his fingers into a claw. "That's when the fangs come out."

"Well the fangs are definitely out!"

Jim Ed stopped painting yet again and that familiar sternness came upon him. "I'm absolutely aware that it's not all your fault," he said. "But right now we're talking about you, aren't we? What's done is done. There's no changing it. It's in the past. If there's any hope of healing your relationship, it's got to start with you."

The old man's words were penetrating. This time I understood all too well what he was saying.

"If you want your wife to start opening up to you again, you have to start creating a safe place for her and begin valuing her. Give her your time and attention. You've got to prize her. You understand what I'm saying?"

I nodded.

"Outside of His own Son, that woman is God's greatest gift to you," he continued. "That is a fact. Your most valuable asset. You want her to feel like the safest place emotionally in the whole world is with you. You gotta make her feel it. To do that you have to start seeing her as God sees her—with priceless value—like God sees you. Over time, when her spirit senses that you truly cherish and value her, she'll start to feel safe again. But it's going take some time. You can't fix in a weekend what took years to break. Then she's got a free will of her own."

"It may be too late," I said feeling sick to my stomach.

"I know this is a ridiculous question to ask, but do you really love Paige?"

"Of course I do. That's not an issue."

"I mean love her enough to do whatever it takes?"

"Jim Ed, I'm terrified. I can't imagine my life without her."

"Then you are going to have to fight, but not like in the past. You have to change your tactics. Everything your flesh screams at you to do, you gotta do the opposite."

"Huh?"

"You have to give up control," said Jim Ed. "Stop trying to control her. Let her go. If you love her, you honor her wishes. Even if that means she walks away. She's free. The more you try to control, the more it drives her away."

I swallowed hard and my legs jiggled up and down nervously.

"After you change your eyes, your heart has to change—get the heart of a warrior. Paige needs to change the way she sees you too. She needs to see the warrior in you—the

David in you. If she does, she'll maybe begin to feel safe with you again."

"I want to be that guy, Jim Ed," I said.

"One of my favorite passages of Scripture is in First Samuel chapter 22. Let me read it to you." He picked up the old, faded Bible again, skimmed through the pages, stopped, and started reading. *"David therefore departed from there and escaped to the cave of Adullam. And everyone who was in distress, everyone who was in debt, and everyone who was discontented gathered to him. So he became captain over them."* Chew on that. David was a mighty warrior and he was a refuge for hurting people. They felt safe with him, and therefore they let him lead. When Paige feels safe with you, she'll let you lead too."

"Just like you," I said. "You've created a safe place for me right here. Maybe you *were* sent."

"Just exercising my gift."

"How do you have so much insight?" I asked.

"Let's just say I've been around the block a few times in my day."

As Jim Ed was placing his Bible back on the cart, a black and white photograph slipped out from the pages and fell to the ground.

"Is that a picture of you and Christina?" I asked as he bent over to pick it up.

"Our wedding day," he said handing it to me.

"Wow," I said, slowly examining the photograph. "She was stunning." Christina was in her wedding dress, her hair twisted above her head, soft and elegant with a much thinner Jim Ed standing tall and proud by her side in a black tuxedo, a grin bigger than the one on Eric's face when he showed me his pix earlier that day in the store. "I'm sure she still is," I added. "You look as handsome now as you did then. More distinguished now."

"Thank you. Yes, she was beautiful."

"Hey, that reminds me," I said handing the old photo back to him. "You're not off the hook. I still want to hear all about her."

"All right," he replied. "But remember, you asked for it."

11

It was 1954 and Jim Ed was home on leave in Pine Grove, Mississippi. He and two of his Army buddies, Willie Taylor and Bo Harris, were all decked out in their uniforms strutting around downtown like they were really something. After downing a bottle of RC Cola in nearly one gulp, Jim Ed looked up—stunned at what he saw across the street.

"Hey man, you see what I see?" he said, wiping his mouth with his forearm.

"I sure do!" said Willie. Bo simply nodded in agreement; he was the quiet one.

"You ever seen anything so fine?" asked Jim Ed. "Where'd she come from?"

"You got me," said Willie. "Never sees her around here before."

"How'd we miss that?" Bo spoke up.

"I don't know," said Jim Ed, "but I gotta meets her."

"Now you know she be way too much woman for you, man," laughed Willie while slapping Jim Ed on the back.

"You think so? You juss watch me and see."

Without saying another word or checking for cars, Jim Ed shot across the street to make his debut. About the same time, an old rusty green and tan '37 Studebaker truck rounded the corner. It didn't run into Jim Ed, Jim Ed ran into it! The crash knocked him backward onto the street with a hard thud. Thankfully he didn't hit his head, as the truck was just creeping along. The *impact did more damage to his ego than his body. He wasn't knocked unconscious, but was shaken up a bit. His uniform got torn from sliding along the asphalt, one elbow was scuffed and bleeding. Though it cost him a few bumps and bruises, all in all, Jim Ed figured it was worth the price. He couldn't have planned a better meeting with Christina.*

Laying on the street, Jim Ed had closed his eyes waiting for the dizziness to stop; and when he opened them, Christina was looking straight down on him with eyes filled with kindness and concern—eyes that were a shade of gold that seemed to blaze against the richness of her smooth, brown skin—the color of coffee with a bit of cream. She was tall and slender, wearing a yellow cotton sundress. Others had gathered around as well, Bo, Willie, and a couple of bystanders, but all Jim Ed could focus on was Christina. And for the first time in his life, he was real glad to be a black man.

"You poor thing, that was terrible," said Christina. "You're bleeding."

"Ah, it's nothing," said Jim Ed, brushing dirt off his shirt and pants as Bo and Willie helped him up. She fished a hand-kerchief from her purse and handed it to him. "I've had closer calls than that in the army" he said dabbing his elbow. "I'm just a little shaken up is all."

"What was you thinking shooting off across the street like that?" teased Willie. "Now I know you is crazy. Done made it home from Korea only to be run over by a truck!"

"I was running across the street to meet her," Jim Ed said cracking a silly grin while holding out his hand toward Christina. "Hi, I'm James Edward Porter, friends call me Jim Ed."

At first she was reserved, didn't quite know how to take him, but then lifted her hand in return. "Hello, I'm Christina

Kenyon, nice to meet you, Jim Ed. You know you are blessed to be alive?"

"I reckon so," he said. When their eyes met something magical happened. It made Jim Ed queasy in his stomach and no other girl had ever done that to him before. "I know you don't know me," he said, "but would you minds if I walked you home?"

Her lips forming into a tender curve, she planted her hands on her hips and sassed back. "Now how could I possibly say no to someone who almost died to meet me? And the word is 'mind' not 'minds'."

"Yes ma'am!" said Jim Ed, trying his best to stay calm on the outside when his heart was doing flips on the inside.

"We have to go to Woolworth's first to pick up a few things for my Papa and Mama. Okay?"

"Whatever you say," said Jim Ed looking over at Bo and Willie and giving them a wink. "Sees, I mean, 'see' you guys later."

"I hears ya," said Willie, slapping him on the back. "I hears ya."

From the first moment Christina and Jim Ed began walking down that road, they both knew something was up. There was an ease between them, like they were meant to be. And they kept on walking together day after day, until a year and a half later, shortly after Jim Ed was honorably discharged from the Army, they were married.

Jim Ed stopped painting for a moment and looked up at me. "Well, that's how we met." He became silent and an air of sadness fell upon him. The ends of his mouth turned down. "Would have been together sixty years come December," he said, hoarseness creeping into his throat.

I frowned back knowing what he was going to say next, feeling crappy that I'd pushed him to talk about her.

"Christina passed on last year."

"I'm real sorry to hear that," I said, my heart sinking. "Real sorry."

"Yeah, me too. That cancer eventually got the best of her. Fought hard till the very end." His eyes became watery and he coughed to clear his throat.

"You don't have to talk about it," I said.

"Now how about you tell me about your Paige. How did ya'll meet?"

I paused, considering whether or not to respond, then closed my eyes and reached twenty-something years in my past. "The first time I really saw Paige was late in my junior year of high school," I said, "it only took one look and I was smitten. I'd seen her before, but this time I really *saw* her, if you know what I mean. It was like a veil lifted from my face and I could see clearly."

"Oh, I know exactly what you mean," said Jim Ed.

"Paige was a year and a half younger than me and literally blossomed over the summer. Before then, I had never paid much attention to her. On that day, however, when she came sashaying down the north hall of our school and our eyes met for the first time that year, like I said, I really saw her. After that there was no one else, period. She was *the* one." I tilted my head back and laughed.

"You're gonna love this, Jim Ed. At the time, I was a big jock on campus, and she was on the dance team that performed with the band at halftimes of the football games. In the huddle on the field during a game while the quarterback was trying to call the plays, I'd be gazing up in the stands watching her. Paige always had that kind of effect on me."

"Sounds like a special gal," said Jim Ed smiling.

"The night of the prom was quite an event. It was pouring down rain, and I was driving my 1972 Chevy Nova Sport to pick up Paige when I took a curve just a little too fast, sending my car sliding through a ditch and into someone's chain-link fence, eventually spinning to a stop in the front yard. No one was home and I was off the road, so undeterred from my goal, I wrote a note, stuck it in the window and left the car in the person's front yard, then hitchhiked in the downpour to Paige's house. You could imagine Paige's face when I showed up at her front door soaking wet. Her father, bless his heart, let us borrow his station wagon to go to the dance. Later that night when Paige dropped me off at home, a cop and my dad were having coffee! My car had been impounded, and I got a ticket for leaving the scene of an accident. Dad was not a happy man, but for Paige, it was well worth it.

For the next year we were inseparable until I graduated and received a football scholarship out of town. The separation was hard. Paige cried because she was sure I would meet someone else and forget her, but like I said, she was the one. As fate would have it, a year later she enrolled in the same college. We were married my junior year. When I blew out my knee, ending my career and dashing my pro-football dreams, it was Paige who kept me going. In fact, she's kept me going many times through the years."

"Sounds like you need to see her again, with fresh eyes," said Jim Ed.

"Yep."

12

After the first day they met, Christina and Jim Ed saw each other almost every day for the next two weeks until he was shipped back overseas. For nearly a year the romance continued via letters. And the letters got spicy at times. They wrote about more than just their enduring love for one another, however. Christina kept Jim Ed up to date on family and happenings around Pine Grove. They shared their dreams and frustrations and wrote often about their racial struggles.

Discrimination was becoming more and more pronounced at home as well as in the military. The more injustice Jim Ed saw in the army, the more bitter he became, until he was eaten alive, filled with hate for the world, for the white man, for the government, and for himself. It amazed him how he could put his life on the line for his country in the war, see so many of his brothers get shot up and blown to bits, yet he couldn't exercise the very freedoms he'd just fought for. To cope, he'd spill out his anger to Christina in his letters, oftentimes ranting on God. Yet, no matter how great the injustice, Christina always responded in love, her letters written in nearly perfect calligraphy.

September 27, 1954

Dearest Jim Ed,

I received your letter last night and was anxious to respond. I'm sorry to hear of your homesickness and of the discrimination you are dealing with. I know it must be a terribly difficult time for you, as it is for all of us. I'm speaking of the discrimination, not the war. I can't imagine how hard that must be on you. If it's any comfort, there are many people here in Pine Grove who love you dearly and miss you greatly, me being the foremost, though I'm sure your Mama would put up a good fight.

I miss you so very much and long for the day of your return. To overcome the void your absence has created, I have filled my nights with study. It helps the time to pass quicker and takes my mind off of missing you.

About our struggle as a people that you wrote about, I want to encourage you to hold on and stand strong in the midst of injustice. It was our brother Fredrick Douglas who said, "One and God make a majority...The soul that is within me no man can degrade...Without a struggle, there can be no progress." Sojourner Truth said, "Truth burns up error." I believe that God is on our side, Jim Ed, and truth will one day burn up error.

Remember the story of Joseph in the Bible? Like us, he too was mistreated when he was sold as a slave and falsely imprisoned. Yet he remained faithful to the cause. In the end, in God's perfect time, Joseph was delivered from that prison of injustice and God put him in a place of leadership over the whole country. If we remain faithful, Jim Ed, in God's time, He too will bring us out! One day there will be black governors and even presidents. And because of Joseph's attitude, when he was finally lifted up to a place of leadership, he ruled not out of anger, but forgiveness and compassion. If Joseph would have lashed out in anger and bitterness, he never would have been promoted. In the end, Joseph forgave those who had mistreated him.

We have to forgive those who mistreat us and stay the course of doing right. But I want you to know that not all white people are misguided and not all black people are innocent. All people, black and white, are created by God equally and equally everyone will face their Creator one day to give an account. Every person, regardless of their color, needs God's mercy and grace.

Enough lecturing. Everyone here says hello. Mama is frying chicken and cooking a batch of butter beans and rice, with mustard greens. Wish you were here to eat some with us. I love you and miss you more than you can ever imagine.

Love,

Christina

P.S. Hope you like the pictures!

Christina's letters were a welcomed break for Jim Ed, and he was crazy in love with her, even if he didn't see eye to eye *with her philosophy about dealing with their struggles. What she wrote sounded great and nice and ideal on paper, but Jim Ed didn't believe that kind of thinking would change anything. What was getting the enemy's attention in the war was pure force! He simply tolerated her idealism and returned home with an increased zeal to wage his own war for equality on American soil. By the time Jim Ed was honorably discharged, he was a powder keg with a short fuse ready to explode. When he finally set foot back in Pine Grove there was a great reunion with family and friends, but as soon as life got back to normal, Jim Ed was confronted with more discrimination and his resentment intensified.*

Outside of her deep faith, Christina's big thing was education. "We have to promote learning as a means to our growth and development," she said. During this time, Christina was honored with a scholarship in education to Jackson State University, a school about an hour and a half up the road from Pine Grove. That scholarship was her only hope for a college education because her family didn't have the money for tuition.

Jim Ed had the G.I. Bill to help with his tuition, but he was caught in a Catch-22 situation. Because he had to go to work, he'd only finished the eighth grade. Jim Ed's family was so poor when he was growing up that at fourteen he had to quit school to help his Papa milk cows on one of the local dairy farms. At that time, because of the poverty of most blacks in the south and having to work, it was hard for many black children to finish school.

Christina had a couple of things going for her. Her dad was the pastor of the Mount Zion Church. that had its own school. Back then, because of the lack of state funding for the black public schools, many of the black churches formed their own schools to educate their children. And because her dad was a pastor, Christina didn't have to quit in order to work.

For a while, Jim Ed drove up to Jackson on Fridays to pick up Christina from school and bring her home for the weekends. One Friday afternoon when they were driving home, he made a little detour to the banks of the Tallahala River.

13

I looked up over Jim Ed's head and couldn't believe my eyes! Behind him, on the trail in the distance, was none other than Eric heading our way. *Really? You gotta be kidding me?* I thought. Hoping he wouldn't recognize me, I turned my back and crunched down on the bench.

"What are you doing?" asked Jim Ed.

"It's that Eric guy I was telling you about," I said. "I don't want him to see me. Don't draw attention to yourself. Look out over the lake or something."

Jim Ed just kept painting, only now holding his head up high in defiance to what I had asked. After a moment or so, I peeked around thinking maybe Eric had passed. Not a chance. He'd already spotted me and was zeroing in.

"Adam!" he called out, jogging right up to the bench between Jim Ed and I. "Twice in one morning! Must be a Divine Appointment!"

"Praise the Lord," I mumbled under my breath.

"What are you doing, man?" he asked taking a swallow of bottled water. "You've been here this whole time?" As he spoke, his back was to Jim Ed never acknowledging him. "You took off in such a hurry back at the store," he said, wiping his mouth with his forearm. "Thought your family needed you?"

"They do."

Eric nodded toward Jim Ed. "Who's this guy?" he asked in a demeaning sort of way. "Is he painting your picture?"

"It's called a portrait actually," I said with an attitude. "Here, let me introduce you. Eric, this is Jim Ed. Jim Ed, this is Eric." From his stool, Jim Ed held out his hand for Eric to shake, but Eric only looked down on the portrait.

"Different," he said cynically. "Doesn't look like Adam at all."

"That's because you're not seeing with the right eyes," Jim Ed replied coolly.

Doesn't look like me? I thought. Now I was really intrigued and stood up to peek.

"Sit down, Adam!" thundered Jim Ed. "It's not time."

"Yes, sir," I said plopping back down.

Eric glanced at me with an expression that said, "Who is this joker? What the heck are you doing here, Adam?"

"It's a gift," I told him.

Eric shook his head. "Sure man, whatever you say." He twisted the cap back on his bottle of water. "Well, gotta scoot. Got a lot on my plate. You know I'm preparing for my big presentation tomorrow at the church?"

I shook my head. "Nope, didn't know that."

"It's been in the bulletin for a month, Adam."

"Oh yeah," I said scratching my head, "Seems I remember something about it now." Once again I lied, now completely certain I was going straight to hell!

"It's called 'How to Raise Champions for God.' Pastor Rick asked me to teach on it. See you tomorrow." At that, he started jogging off.

"Eric," Jim Ed called out kindly but sternly.

Eric stopped and turned around. "Yeah?"

"How's that little problem you've got with your computer?"

Eric looked perplexed. "What are you talking about, dude?"

"I think you know," said Jim Ed.

"No. I really don't," said Eric, jogging off again, this time faster.

"We're as sick as our secrets, Eric." Jim Ed yelled out. "You know…those things that are secretly tormenting you." Eric never turned around but slowed to almost a stop keeping his legs moving in place. I didn't know what was happening but felt the electricity of the moment. "God wants to set you free, Eric," Jim Ed continued. "He really loves you. You can stop the performance."

Eric slowed and then turned his body around again to face Jim Ed. I thought for sure he was going to blow a gasket or something, but instead sorrowfulness dropped across his face like a wet blanket and a fist-size knot rose up in his throat. His legs became still and he swallowed hard.

"God wants to free you from your diluted self and the lies," Jim Ed said warm and inviting like he had done with me, "so you can become the authentic man you were created to be."

Eric glanced at me, back at Jim Ed, back at me, then back at Jim Ed again. I could tell he was wrestling in his mind, didn't want to expose himself. Just then, his whole body began to shake. He dropped his water bottle and fell to the ground on his knees.

Jim Ed walked over, knelt down and gently touched Eric's shoulder. "God wants you to know that you are His, Eric," said Jim Ed. "Never doubt that."

I couldn't hear the rest of the conversation, but I could see the impact it was having on Eric. It was as if Jim Ed and Eric were the only two people in the area. Their conversation was intense, and Eric covered his face as tears streamed down his face. Then Jim Ed said, "Now go in peace and prepare well for your presentation tomorrow. Some young parents need to hear what you have to say."

"Thank you," Eric said, rising to his feet. He turned to me with a contrite look on his face and nodded like an unspoken sign of acceptance. The pasted-on grin was gone and the Eric I was seeing now was someone I could probably spend some time with. He then reached out his hand toward Jim Ed. Jim Ed grasped his hand, holding it tightly for a few long seconds before releasing it. Eric turned and took off down the trail.

Jim Ed resumed his painting as if nothing happened while I sat there amazed at what had just transpired before me. A warm peace filled my heart as Jim Ed continued his story.

14

A gravel road wound from the bridge down to the Tallahala River's edge and the two of them were sitting in Jim Ed's parked truck. It was a place where the local coloreds came to fish, swim, and picnic. The sun was beginning to set and he and Christina were gazing out over the water. "Ain't That a Shame" by Fats Domino was playing on the truck's scratchy radio. Christina was swaying, tapping her fingers to the beat on Jim Ed's thigh. He let the song finish then turned the radio off. The only sounds were the whine of the locusts in concert with the churning river water where it flowed over some fallen trees. Jim Ed pulled Christina closer and tenderly kissed her on the lips. The aroma of her perfume and hair combined with the moistness of her lips and the softness of her skin overpowered him. He buried his face in her hair and breathed in her essence.

"It sure is beautiful out here," he whispered in her ear. "I thought about this place a lot when overseas."

Christina pushed him away. "I thought you only thought about me," she said, her lips forming a silly smile.

"You know I missed you the most."

"Just making sure. A woman has to know about these things."

"That reminds me," said Jim Ed, reaching into the truck's glove compartment for something. "Close your eyes. I have a surprise for you. And don't you peek."

Christina squeezed her eyes shut.

"Okay, now open them."

In his hands, Jim Ed was holding up a silver heart-shaped locket on a chain.

"It was my grandmother's," he said. "She passed it down to my Mama who passed it on to me so I could give it to you."

"Oh, Jim Ed, it's beautiful!"

"Look Christina," said Jim Ed. "I'm not too good at fancy words, so I'm just gonna says what's on my mind. …Christina, from the first day we met, I knew you was the one for me. And I…I…hope you think I'm the one for you. When overseas, nearly all I could think about was getting back home to you. It was the thoughts of you that helped keep me safe."

"And a lot of prayers from me and your family," added Christina.

"Yes, of course. But, what I'm trying to say is…Christina… will you marry me? …Before you answer, I have another surprise. I got me a good job in Jackson now. Start the first of next month. Because of working on trucks in the Army, I got hired as a mechanic at the Sears & Roebuck Auto Center. The pay is decent so I can at least put a roof over our heads till you finish school and we can get something better and—"

Christina placed one finger over Jim Ed's mouth. "Shhh," she said, moving her body closer and cuddling up under his arm. There was a long silence and Jim Ed was starting to get nervous. He'd already been sweating.

"Mrs. Christina Porter," she said. "I like the sound of that."

"So that means yes?"

"What do you think? Of course it means yes."

"Yeeeee Haaaa!" Jim Ed let out a holler so loud that tradition says it could be heard all the way to Osyka twenty miles down the road.

"Jim Ed," Christina said, "Calm down. I will marry you, but there is one condition though."

Jim Ed's holler quickly became a whimper. "Yes ma'am?"

"You have to let me teach you. Because you're a veteran now you can take the new G.E.D. test and then you can go to college on the G.I. Bill. You have to take advantage of the opportunity, Jim Ed."

"What?"

"Hey, you think I'm joking? This is no game to me. I'm serious. You let me work with you and one day you will go to college too. You have so much to offer, Jim Ed."

Jim Ed turned his head away from Christina and looked out the truck window thinking about her proposal. "All right, I guess so," he said, turning his head back. "Mrs. Porter-to-be, it's a deal."

"You promise, Jim Ed? Because I know you're a man of your word. If you let me down, I'll be so disappointed because I know you can do it. You've got great gifts in you that God wants to develop, Jim Ed."

"I promise."

"It's not going to be easy."

"I said I promise."

"Now you can holler," said Christina.

"Yeeeee Haaaa!"

15

Jim Ed cleared his throat. "Sure do miss her. Sometimes I get so lonely, but not lonely from being by myself. I see a lot of people—have many friends. I get lonely for my life partner, my soul mate. When Christina died, it was like the best part of me died right along with her. You have to understand, we went through a whole life together and after each battle we fought and won, we became that much stronger. It's great to have someone in the foxholes of life with you. She was the best thing that ever happened to me outside of the good Lord Himself. You know, in the beginning, our relationship was mostly about our physical attraction and passion—all the fluff of infatuation. As we grew older, all that slowed down. But you know what?"

"What?" I said, sitting up on the edge of the bench.

"Infatuation gave way to something much better… authentic love. You see, when I saw my life's partner coming through for me again and again, standing by my side, getting dirty with me in the foxholes of life, my love for her grew that much deeper. Wasn't always easy. Had to push through some hard times. I remember when our girl Tallah died. Got the measles just two years before the vaccine. Two years! Only eight years old, my baby girl was just beginning to live. Can't imagine the heartache. Something you never get over.

Just learn to live with it. Still hurts after all these years. I was so mad at God.

"Christina went into deep grief too, but she never got angry with God though she had a ton of questions for Him. I thought for sure that tragedy was going to be the end of my faith and maybe us, but just the opposite happened. Jesus met us and carried us. The only way I can explain… it's supernatural. Sometimes tragedy drives couples apart, but Christina and I got closer, the bond between us stronger.

"As time passed, even though she was still the most beautiful thing my eyes ever did see, her outer shell started to mean less and less because now I was in love with her true being, her character. And I tell you what, that woman had some kind of character. She stuck by my side through thick and thin, pushing me, encouraging me. After a while, our souls just meshed, became one. In the beginning, we were one in body, but as we grew together, we became one in spirit. A lot of people get married and become one in body, but they never become one in spirit.

"When I first married Christina, I felt honored that she married me—couldn't imagine that out of everyone in the whole world she actually picked me to spend the rest of her life with. Think about it. That's some kind of honor—a person picking you to spend their whole life with. I suppose I never really got over it—the honor of it all."

"You were fortunate to have found that kind of love in life," I said. "Some people never do."

"You sure are right. I was truly fortunate. This may surprise you, but you know what I miss the most?"

I shrugged my shoulders.

"The hugs. They were the best part. I long to touch Christina's soft skin and to smell her sweetness. My favorite parts of the day were in the mornings and the evenings when we'd hug in the bed. And when she'd be standing in the kitchen, I'd walk up behind her and wrap my arms around her from behind. Squeeze her tight and nibble on her neck and ears and smell her hair. Her scent was like a drug. I tell you, it'd put me in a state. Sometimes I can still smell her around the house, almost as if she were standing right in front of me. This morning I was standing at the kitchen sink, and I swear I could smell her. You know what I'm talking about—that unique scent that each person has? Every day that goes by, however, her scent fades from the house a little bit more. Sometimes I'll walk around the house like some crazy old man, sniffing pillows and towels and things, trying desperately to recapture her scent."

"That's not crazy, Jim Ed."

"Whenever I touched her and took in her scent, it gave me energy for living. And you know what else we'd do? … Almost every night Christina would sit down at one end of the couch and I'd sit down on the other and she'd put her feet up in my lap and I'd rub them while we watched TV. She loved me rubbing her feet, but to tell you the truth, I think I loved rubbing them more. It was real calming for me…we didn't have to be going out on the town all the time in order to be content. We were just as happy sitting on the couch being together. I'm gonna tell you something else that I know you're not going to believe." Jim Ed grinned like a little child.

"As we got older, the loving got better. Most of the time, it was so good we couldn't hardly believe it ourselves. I tell young people, you can't compare a one-night stand to the loving that comes from years of real love and partnership—loving when you're one in spirit. There's no comparison. Of course, to have that kind of loving, you have to really value your mate. I like to tell young men, if you want your wife to respond, you have to treat her like the queen she is. You make her feel really special...and I guarantee she'll respond." He sat his brush down and again looked up at the sky. "But I still miss the hugs the most."

My head dropped. "I know Paige needed my affection," I said. "She'd been asking me to open up to her and let her in."

Jim Ed's eyes again fixed onto mine with that now familiar stare. Obviously he didn't want me to miss the point he was about to make.

"There's something special about touching the ones you love," he said. "Never forget to touch the people you love because one day they may not be here. Touch them. Smell them. Take in their essence and energy. So many take the people in their lives for granted—don't know what they have until they're gone." A single tear rolled down his cheek and he made no attempt to wipe it away. "I'd give just about anything to hold my Christina one more time. She was my best friend, my very best friend."

For the next minute or two Jim Ed painted in silence, no doubt reliving distant memories of him and Christina.

I wiped the tears from my eyes.

16

"Another thing an artist must understand," said Jim Ed, popping out of his trance, ready to get back to the business of painting, "is the role that light plays. It's important in order to produce a realistic work. You have to figure out how to "light" the image you're going to paint and how the variation of light falling on the image affects it, then how to capture the light on the canvas or paper. It's harder than you may think. Takes some skill. Capturing just the right light, on just the right spots on the canvas, is vital. You know why?"

I scratched my head. "I would guess that light probably has something to do with setting the tone."

"Partially," he said. "Light not only creates the atmosphere that you're painting, but it reveals and illuminates. And there are different kinds of light—direct light, reflected light, and shadow. Yet in all aspects, the job of light in painting is to reveal something about the work—something that the artist wants to bring out."

"Oooookay," I said slowly, curious of where he was going with this one. By now I was quite certain it was somewhere other than painting.

"There are things the light wants to reveal. Areas of your life. The problem is light is painful until you adjust. Men love darkness because light reveals truth about them and it stings.

"You know how I said that you are made up of seventy percent water and you need water to survive? Well, just like we need water to survive, we also need light to survive. It helps us see and gives us the energy and warmth we require to exist. Just as sure as I am painting this portrait, our ole earth and all the life on it would gradually die without light. But you know what else light does?"

"You've got me thinking."

"Light doesn't just reveal, it consumes darkness. When you walk into a dark room what's the first thing you do?"

"Turn on the light."

"And when you do, that darkness just skedaddles right on outta there, doesn't it? Darkness can't take the light."

"So what's the punch line?"

"Well, if you are going to have a beautiful life portrait, Adam, a masterpiece, you must let light shine in the right spots on your life canvas. It reveals things that need to be chipped away—everything that isn't the David in you. That's what it means to live in the light. For some folk, the atmosphere of their life painting is dominated by the gloomy shadows of negative thinking—bitterness, prejudice, arrogance, jealousy, anger, selfishness, hatred—even hatred for themselves—you name it, all sorts of poisonous attitudes. These poisonous attitudes flourish in the darkness, so it's imperative to open up and let light shine on our canvas to reveal those dark spots.

"If I see that this painting in front of me needs more light, then I can add some strategic brushstrokes and change the whole mood of it. When a person lets God brushstroke His light on their canvas, the whole mood of their life changes too. God's light reveals truth and helps us see in ways we've never seen before. And no matter how dark your life may seem, when you receive His truth and walk with God, He will always give you the light you need for where you are, even if you're in a place of pain and difficulty. Can be painful at times though, letting the light reveal things we don't like about ourselves, but we need His light to survive."

"You sure you're not a preacher?" I smirked.

"Nope, just a friend who wishes to pass down some of what I've learned through the years, to make somebody else's journey a little less bumpy before I pass on. Won't be long now."

"Don't talk like that. You're not dying."

"At my age, I think I am. In truth, we all are. I'm just a lot closer than you...probably. But you never know. You could go before me. Nobody knows when their time will be up. David prayed, 'teach us to number our days that we might gain a heart of wisdom.' All of our days are numbered, Adam, and I've heard Jesus calling my name. He and my sweetheart will be meeting me."

"You like David, don't you," I said.

"Yes sir, I do," said Jim Ed. "You see David is an Old Testament shadow of Christ. Really, the David in you, the masterpiece God wants to bring out, is Jesus. God wants to form us into the image of His Son. The more God shines His light on us and chips away at us, the more we look like Jesus."

"So how do I do all this?" I asked, my eyes misting up. "You know...let God's light in? Let Him make me more like Jesus?"

"Again, it's simple Adam, but it's not easy. First, you have to know your identity and then live your life in desperate dependence on Him. See God as your source for everything. I mean, you can't do a thing without Him, not a single thing. Feeding on His word and fellowship with Him becomes not just a religious duty or discipline. It becomes your lifeline, your very food for survival. He's your source for the breath of life when you get out of the bed in the morning. He's the source for your righteousness and your growth. He's your source for provision, both materially and emotionally. Bottom line is you can't do life without Him. He's your only hope.

"On your own you're weak, Adam, but understanding your weakness becomes your greatest strength when your security is in Him, when you are desperately dependent on Him. Don't pursue greatness or happiness, Adam, pursue God. That is the key to everything. When He is your security, supernatural things can happen."

Jim Ed stopped talking to search for something in his cart.

"May I see your Bible?" I asked him. "I'd like to look at it."

"Sure," he said, "Love for you to." He took it off his cart and handed it to me.

As I held the old, faded leather book in my hands, I realized this was more than just any old Bible. Flipping through the tattered pages, some were taped together, others were folded. There were hundreds of notes scribbled in the margins. Verses were circled and underlined in a myriad of colors. This Bible was a testament to Jim Ed's life. It was a part of who he was. Paige and I had started our marriage with God in the center, but over time, the pressing issues of life came up and choked out the things of God.

"I know this may seem elementary to you, Adam," said Jim Ed, "but God's Word is the light that He uses to shine into our lives. It brings healing to our wounds. He allows us to see with fresh eyes. It's how He chips away everything that isn't David. It's God's love letter to us and a life map. If you want to get to know God, get to know His Word. Most Christians have heard that since they were knee high to a grasshopper, still they feed on everything else but God's Word. Always seeking some new spiritual experience or revelation, but all you need to guide your life is right there in that book."

On the inside of the back cover, I found a handwritten note from Christina in perfect calligraphy. I read it out loud.

December 20th, 1966

Jim Ed,

Remember, your security is in Him, not in your apparent success. As you continue to go to Him for your security, He speaks and leads you. You see it as a weakness. God sees it as a strength. Maybe you being a little "hungry" is what's needed for your calling, like your thorn in the flesh. You being "desperately dependant" on God is your calling as a man. Do you know how few people hear from God and then act on it? Your obedience to His calling is trusting Him every day, step by step. He is real and He is using you. Praise His name. In that place of going to God for fulfillment, He gives you the gift of Him speaking to you. I'm proud of you, man of God!

Love, Christina

I closed the Bible and handed it back to Jim Ed. Two single tears streamed down his cheeks.

"Like my Christina said, you have to be 'hungry' for God, desperately dependent on Him." Jim Ed wiped his eyes. "Most folks don't want to know the truth. Got itching ears. But a person has to make a decision to walk in the light. I remember the very first day I made the decision to really walk in the light. My life has never been the same since. I can tell you about it if you like."

"I'm not moving."

Jim Ed reached up and tightened the clips that were securing the watercolor paper. Then he bent over the painting and blew some puffs of air over a couple of spots. When he finished blowing, he again reached back into his past.

17

On the next Saturday after Jim Ed proposed, he, Willie, and Bo, decided to walk into town and catch a movie at the theater on Main Street. They hadn't driven because Mama Porter had taken the truck shopping. The three young men walked along the road and crossed Line Creek, which was a natural division that separated the black sections from the white sections. Once across the creek, they didn't walk through any white neighborhoods, but stayed alongside the main highway that led into town. It was only a couple miles into downtown where they were headed.

After a while, they walked up on Boyd's Phillip 66 service station and store and decided to cut through the parking lot to another street. It was a cinderblock building painted white, but the white was flaking and was stained orange from the cars kicking up dust in the parking lot. Out front were two faded green and yellow gas pumps. Next to the store was a grimy garage with tires and junk stacked everywhere. No one was getting gas, and the store was empty other than the four hundred-pound Mr. Boyd who was wearing a pair of overalls with no shirt underneath, sitting out front in a rusty patio chair. There was an old, torn-down car in the garage with a greasy mechanic leaning over it. Between the store and the garage were six white guys drinking beer and hanging out around a couple of pickup trucks. Jim Ed and his friend's first mistake had been cutting through the parking lot.

"Well lookie what we got coming here," one of the white guys said in a loud voice, half drunk, while adjusting his John Deere cap and spitting a stream of tobacco juice on the ground. Lewis was his name and he took a step toward Jim Ed and his friends. *"Where you niggers think you're going?"*

"Keep walking," Jim Ed whispered to Bo and Willie. *"Just ignore them."*

When Jim Ed said that, the guy in the John Deere cap stepped directly in front of them. The three young black men tried to step around him, but the other five whites blocked the path with their arms folded across their chests. It was the three against six.

"I asked you a question, boy. Where you niggers think you're going?"

"Look," Jim Ed said. *"We don't want no trouble. We're just going over to town to watch a movie."*

"Well it looks like you done gone and found yourself some trouble, now didn't you?"

"We juss passing through," Willie said.

"Yes you are. The problem is...this here is private property. No niggers allowed. Now how long you boys been living around here? You should know that."

"We're sorry. We weren't thinking," Jim Ed offered.

"You right about that. Caint you see that sign over there?" he said while pointing to a sign above the store's door that was hard to read because the red letters were faded and the white background blended with the building.

"I see it now, but didn't before."

"Read it to me."

Jim Ed gritted his teeth. Bo started to say something smart, but Jim Ed held his arm out for him to stay quiet.

"Read it to me, I said—if you can."

"I can read."

"Well then do it, boy. Go on."

In the war Jim Ed had put down guys much bigger and tougher than this slimy piece of flesh. All three of them had. The only thing that made this guy strong was his five buddies standing there with him. Humiliated and embarrassed, Jim Ed read the sign. "No Niggers or Dogs allowed! Dogs can wait outside. Niggers will be shot!"

"Hey Lewis, you ever see one that black?" one of the other guys said, pointing to Willie.

"He looks like one of them monkeys in the zoo, don't you think?" Lewis replied. "Hey, maybe they escaped. We need to call the zoo and find out. Maybe there's a reward for their capture."

"I got me a wild hog cage back home we could put 'em in," another one said. All six cracked up laughing. Then, just that quick, their faces went from wise guys to rage. Lewis stepped up to Willie, his veins popping out of his red neck. "Don't you ever set foot on this property again. You hear me, nigger?" At that, he spit another stream of tobacco, but this time it landed on Willie's shoe.

"You not God," Willie shouted. "You can't spit on me!" Something broke in Willie and he pushed Lewis in the chest. When he did, all hell broke loose as the six white guys jumped on them. Everybody was swinging and taking punches. In the midst of the mayhem, Bo and Jim Ed grabbed Willie to run, something they should have done first, but as they were taking off, Lewis picked up an old hubcap that was leaning against a stack of tires, and brought it down across Willie's skull, slicing it wide open, knocking him to the ground.

Mr. Boyd, who'd been sitting there watching the whole thing and had already called the cops, fired a gunshot in the air. "Party's over fellas," he hollered. "Cops on the way. Now break it up." Everybody stepped back and Willie lay still on the ground, blood everywhere.

Lewis put his boot on Willie's back and shook him. "Get up, nigger. Now ya'll get on out of here." But Willie didn't move.

Jim Ed leaned over and tried to get him up. "Come on, Willie, get up. We gotta go," he told him. He shook him again, but Willie still didn't move. Then Bo shook him with the same results and the two young black men looked at each other frozen with shock, not believing what they saw before them.

"He ain't dead," said Lewis. "I didn't hit him hard enough. He's faking like all niggers do." Lewis flipped Willie over with his foot. "Get up I said!"

But when Willie rolled on his back, his eyes were wide open and fixed. Jim Ed and Bo's lifelong friend was lying there dead. "This can't be happening," Jim Ed thought. In the background sirens could be heard and Lewis started getting fidgety. He turned to his friends and shouted. "Those niggers attacked us. And that one tried to kill me. I was just defending myself. Ya'll all saw it."

While the five other whites consoled Lewis, Jim Ed and Bo stood silent in the background. They'd thought about running, but figured they didn't do anything wrong. Plus, where'd they run to anyway? Within what seemed like a few seconds, two police cars whipped in the parking lot and three deputies hopped out with guns drawn. Without even asking the first question, they pushed Bo and Jim Ed to the ground, jerked their hands behind their backs, and clamped the handcuffs down on their wrists. "You're under arrest," they shouted.

"For what?" Jim Ed hollered back.

"Assault and battery, instigating a riot, trespassing and disturbing the peace," the deputy answered, shoving Jim Ed's head into the ground. Under his breath the deputy mumbled, "Stupid niggers."

The two were thrust into separate police cars and whisked off to the jailhouse, while the police never laid a hand on any of the other guys. Blood was running from a gash beneath Jim Ed's eye and the salt from his sweat caused it to burn. It was only a short distance to the police station, yet the ride seemed to last forever. People walking down the street and driving by gaped at them like they were criminals and were the scum of the earth. But all Jim Ed and Bo could think about was Willie.

They were locked up in a jail cell that reeked with the stench of alcohol and vomit. Rights were virtually non-existent—no phone call, no visitors, nothing. Lying on that stone-cold bunk all night Jim Ed's soul ached for the loss of his friend and his mind brooded over the injustice of it all. Bo cried himself to sleep. It should have been clear to anyone with a kernel of sense that they were innocent and Willie had been murdered in cold blood.

After spending the night in jail without talking to anyone except each other, to their surprise, around ten the next morning the sheriff swung open the jail door and told Jim Ed and Bo to get out.

"So, that's it?" Jim Ed asked the sheriff. "What about Lewis? You know he killed Willie in cold blood. Everybody saw it!"

"Now that's where you are wrong. Eyewitnesses said there was a fight plain and simple." The sheriff grabbed Jim Ed's arm and squeezed it tight. "Son, because Mr. Boyd said you boys weren't lookin' for trouble, I'm letting you go. If you know *what's good for you, you'll just keep that big mouth of yours shut because I can easily put you right back in that cell and lock the door. You hear me? Hell, I'm doing you a favor, son. You ought to be thanking me."*

18

For the next several days, Jim Ed couldn't talk to anyone about the incident, not Christina, not Mama Porter, not Bo or anybody. He was out of his mind with grief and rage. But it was when he saw Willie laying in his casket that he cracked. And upon hearing the wails of his people when they put him in the ground, Jim Ed knew what he had to do.

The rest of the afternoon, during the post-funeral dinner at the church, Jim Ed quietly contemplated his plan. Christina realized that something was up and it was more than just grief over losing Willie.

"I'm so sorry about Willie," she said. "It was such a tragic thing and I know you are hurting, Jim Ed." She put her arm around his waist and pulled herself close. The two walked out of the fellowship hall into the yard outside. Despite the sadness all around, kids were running around playing.

"Not that long ago Willie and I were doing the same thing," Jim Ed said, glancing at the kids.

"What are you thinking?" Christina asked. "It's like you're in another world and won't let me in."

Jim Ed stared at her coldly. "My best friend was murdered, Christina. Of course I'm in another world."

"I'm sorry, honey," she said caressing the back of his head with her fingers. "I just want to help you."

"You can help by leaving me alone!"

"Jim Ed, I know you, and I know that's not the real you speaking. You're up to something and I have an uneasiness in my spirit about it."

As they walked, the sun began to set. Soon it would be dark and Jim Ed could move ahead with his plan. "Did you know that Willie saved my life one time?" he asked.

"You never told me that," said Christina.

"Yep. He sure did. I was eleven and a bunch of us was swimming over at Miller's bluff. We liked to jump off the bluffs into the water. The water was muddy and when I jumped my foot rammed right through this rotten log under the water. It bruised and cut my foot, but worse, my foot was stuck and the log was set deep in the mud. I flung around underwater trying to free myself, but my foot wouldn't budge. I gave out of air thinking I was going to die, but right when I could sense my body fading out of consciousness, I felt somebody's arm. He shook the log over and over. Finally, my foot slipped free. It was Willie. He had jumped in to rescue me. If he hadn't done that, I would have been buried long time ago."

Christina didn't say a word, but squeezed him tightly.

"Willie deserves justice and the law is sure not going to give it to him. So somebody has to. I owe him." When Jim Ed said that, he immediately realized he'd given too much information.

"Jim Ed, what are you thinking?"

"Look, Christina, I really have to go now. I'll see you tomorrow," he said, pulling away.

Christina jerked him back to herself. "It's not like you to just up and leave. Something's up and you need to tell me right now before you do something you're gonna regret!"

"Don't feel like talking right now." At that Jim Ed ripped himself out of Christina's embrace and walked briskly toward his old truck in the field where the cars were parked. Christina followed.

"So, you're just going to leave me like that?"

"I have to go. You can get a ride with your daddy."

"Jim Ed, I'm worried about you—about what you're thinking of doing! No good's going to come of it!"

"Don't worry, Christina, I've got a plan."

"A plan? You've been planning?"

"I know what I'm doing. Sometimes a man's gotta do what he's gotta do. It's that simple!"

"Jim Ed!" she screamed through tears. "You don't know what you're doing! You're not thinking right! You need to cool down!"

"Oh, I'm perfectly aware of what I'm doing."

"Listen to me! You can't fight evil with evil! Evil will win every time."

"Well your God sure doesn't do anything! That's for sure! Where's the justice for Willie? Answer that. Why didn't God do something?"

"God didn't kill Willie, Jim Ed, an evil man did!"

Christina latched onto Jim Ed's arm and jerked him to a stop. He looked down at her indifferently. "Jim Ed," she pleaded in desperation. "You can't do this. Please, if you love me. You won't do this! Please...for me."

By now, others in the church yard had turned to see the commotion they were making. With thoughts of Willie in his mind, Jim Ed simply turned back toward his truck. Christina released her grip and took her engagement locket from her neck.

"Here," she said in a whisper. "I can't marry you. If this is the man you are, if this is who you've become, then I won't marry you." The locket fell from her hands into his. She collapsed to her knees and sobbed. Jim Ed opened the truck door, slid inside, and drove away.

19

Jim Ed's story was like watching a movie or reading a novel. Though my neck and shoulders were beginning to get stiff, I wasn't moving until the man painting my portrait finished his story.

Grinding the gears on his truck, Jim Ed sped away toward his Mama's house. Once there, he jumped out, darted up the steps, through the screen door, and pulled out of a pillow case the old Smith & Wesson revolver handed down to him from his father. Lewis lived alone in the woods about five miles outside of town. The plan was to park his truck some distance away, hide out in the woods and wait as long as it took. When Jim Ed was sure no one else was around he would go up to his house and confront him face to face and take justice into his own hands. He couldn't just shoot Lewis from a distance. It had to be up close and personal. Jim Ed wanted him to see his pain. He wanted to, he needed to, watch him suffer. Lewis had to pay for what he had done to Willie.

As Jim Ed sped along, he was bent on killing Lewis; but then, totally unexpected, in a split second, something happened that could only be described as a miracle. When he left the church, nothing was changing his mind, not even his beloved

Christina. Yet as he turned on the gravel road that led to Lewis' place, a light shone on Jim Ed. A strange and awful uneasiness came over him and then a Voice spoke from deep inside his core, "If you do this, Jim Ed, your life is over. There's a better way. This is a turning point for you." The inner Voice was so strong it seemed almost audible. Jim Ed couldn't explain it other than God because he knew it wasn't coming from him. He hadn't been thinking like that. The Voice was contrary to his state of mind. It was clear—he had the power to choose, and that choice would determine his destiny.

His whole body began to tremble and his heartbeat became rapid. Sweat oozed from his pores. Jim Ed slowed down and eased the truck off to the side of the road. Parked there, he gazed down at Christina's locket lying on the seat next to him while the words she'd spoken over the past year came flooding into his mind. He adjusted the rearview mirror so he could better see himself.

"Jim Ed, look at what you are becoming," the Voice said. "You were willing to hurt Christina and your family, possibly endanger them and go to jail or get killed, just to satisfy your rage. Is this what Willie would want if he were alive? Is this what you really want?"

At that moment, right there in the truck, the fog lifted and Jim Ed's mind became crystal clear. The light was on. The darkness was revealed and dispelled and he knew that Christina was right. God's grace poured over him, washing him, filling his soul with peace. A plan was laid out before him. Yes, it was his duty to fight the terrible injustice and evil of prejudice, but not by responding with aggression and violence. Getting even with Lewis would only bring judgment on him and his family.

Jim Ed had to turn his anger over to God and somehow, with God's strength, fight evil with the power of good, by becoming the best man he could, developing his faculties and striving to be the man God made him to be—a warrior fighting injustice by proving they were wrong and by making progress despite the struggle. That is what he would be held responsible for. He would become the man God created him to be, for Willie's sake, for Christina's, and for himself.

Jim Ed's head dropped down on the steering wheel and he wept. He wept hard, long heaves, emptying himself. "God," he cried. "Take me and all my hate! If You are really who Christina says You are, then please forgive me and fill me with strength to fight and help me do the right thing!" He opened the revolver's cylinder, dumped the bullets in his hand, and tossed them out the window. When the bullets left his hand, Jim Ed released a long, drawn-out sigh of relief and it felt as if a ten-ton weight had been lifted off his back. He turned the truck around and headed back to the church.

On the way, Jim Ed met Mr. Kenyon and Bo who were racing to find him to try and talk some sense into him. They pulled their vehicles side by side. Through wet eyes, Jim Ed explained to them his experience and was now headed back to the church cemetery and then on to see Christina.

"It was the Holy Spirit, son," said Mr. Kenyon. "As soon as Christina told us you'd gone, everybody at the church gathered and prayed that God would intervene. I believe He did."

Back at the church cemetery, it was dark and Jim Ed stood beside Willie's grave alone among the flowers, red clay, and mosquitoes. "Willie, my brother," he said. "I'm sorry for letting you down and for not covering your back. Please forgive me. You *know that I want justice for you with all my heart, but I'm seeing that the best justice I can give is to fight this thing with goodness and being the man God made me to be. I promise you, Willie, I will live this life for the both of us and make you real proud. I promise. I will see you later, brother. That's a promise too."*

When he turned into Christina's driveway that night after visiting Willie's grave, she was waiting for him on the front porch swing. She had heard the news from her daddy. The moment she saw him she flew off the porch to meet him. Leaning against the truck, they held each other tightly. Then Jim Ed took the locket out of his pocket and slid it back over her head. "I'm sorry for the way I treated you today. I was wrong, and I never want to treat you like that again."

"I'm so proud of you, Jim Ed," Christina said through tears of joy.

Jim Ed pulled her face close to his. "You have to help me do this, Christina. Help me to fight the good fight and be the man God made me to be. I can't do it without you."

"We're a team. You and me and the Lord. 'A threefold cord is not quickly broken,' Ecclesiastes 4:12. We're going to make it."

"You're an incredible woman, Christina," Jim Ed said, gently kissing her lips.

It was a defining moment for him.

20

Jim Ed's powerful story left me feeling moved with respect for him and a longing for a life partner like he had with Christina. My eyes were opened to what could be between me and Paige. It would take God's help, a miracle perhaps, but it was now something I knew I wanted and was willing to fight for.

Following the incident, Jim Ed laid low for a while because he knew the cops were watching him. Fortunately, he started his job in Jackson less than two weeks later and he never saw Lewis again. That is, until nearly a half century later. Lewis tracked Jim Ed down using the Internet and asked if they could meet. At first Jim Ed didn't want to have anything to do with him. He had no desire to reopen old wounds, but Christina convinced Jim Ed it was the right thing to do, that it was what Christ would do. The two men met one afternoon at the very park where he and Adam were now.

Jim Ed was not prepared for what he saw—a man who had lived an entire life filled with regret, eaten alive by bitterness and guilt. Lewis was thin and frail and wheelchair-bound. His skin had a yellowish-pale tint, and he couldn't breathe without the aid of an oxygen tank. His daughter, Lydia, who had accompanied him, pushed his wheelchair to the bench and then waited in a rental car while he and Jim Ed talked. What got Jim Ed the most, though, were Lewis' eyes—eyes filled with absolute terror. Lewis was a dying man who was extremely afraid.

"Mr. Porter," Lewis said, his entire body trembling as he sucked in prolonged breaths of oxygen between sentences. "I don't know how to say this, but I am sincerely sorry for what happened that day. I was young and foolish. I've prayed thousands of times for God's forgiveness over the years," he continued, "but it would mean so much if somehow you could find it in your heart to forgive me. I'm a dying man who wants to make things right so I can have a bit of peace before I go."

After all those years of putting the incident behind him and moving on with his life, Jim Ed felt the anger beginning to rise up inside him again. Just seeing Lewis' face, even though it was now withered and creased, brought the past fully and painfully into the present. "It's not me that you need to be asking for forgiveness, but God and Willie. He's the one you murdered in cold blood. And you got away with it!"

"I've been to Willie's grave countless times," Lewis responded. "I've asked him to forgive me over and over. I've asked God for forgiveness so many times...but can never get any peace in my heart. That's why I've come to you. You would know what Willie would do. Would he forgive me? I need to know. Can you forgive me? Maybe if you can, then I'll believe that Willie can and God can."

"You talk about making things right," said Jim Ed. "Well what about Willie, Lewis? He didn't have a chance to make things right or to have a bit of peace before he went. He didn't even have time to pray to God like you did." Jim Ed raised his voice and

spoke forcefully. "But I can assure you of this; Willie is in Heaven, and he is at peace!" He wagged his finger in Lewis' face. "And to tell you the truth, I don't know what Willie would do. Do you realize how much pain you caused? The dreams you snuffed out? If you are so set on making things right, I'll drive you to the police station and you can turn yourself in! How about that?" Tears were streaming down Lewis' face. "I'll tell you something else I bet you didn't know. I came within a trigger's breath of killing you." Lewis looked up at Jim Ed somewhat taken aback. "Yes, that's right. Don't look so surprised. I got my pistol; put it in my truck, and after Willie's funeral drove out to your old place with the full intention of putting a bullet through your skull."

"Why didn't you?" Lewis struggled. "You should have. It would have saved me a lot of misery. Believe me, not a day goes by that I don't relive what I did. Sometimes I lay awake all night long as the scene from that day replays over and over in my mind like a broken record that I can't turn off! If I could go back and make things right I would. I was wrong. We were wrong. No one deserved to be treated like that."

"You know why I didn't kill you that day?" said Jim Ed. "Because I realized that if I would have shot you, I would have ended up just like you, eaten alive with bitterness and guilt my whole life, only to end up old and pathetic, full of regret, just like you are now! You know what? You got exactly what you deserved—a life of misery!" After he said that, Jim Ed turned and walked away.

"No!" Lewis cried out through a rasping cough. "Please," he coughed again, "don't leave!"

Jim Ed could hear him wheezing for breath and when he turned around, he noticed that Lewis' breathing tube had fallen out and was lying on the ground. Lewis was leaning forward in his wheelchair clawing frantically for it but couldn't reach it. Jim Ed walked over to him, picked it up, and handed it to him. Lewis shoved it back into his nostrils and sucked in a long extended gasp of oxygen.

"Listen to me, please," he said, grabbing hold of Jim Ed's arm. Sweat had beaded up on his brow and his whole body was shaking. "Everything happened so fast that day. You've got to believe me. I picked up that hubcap without even thinking. I never intended to kill him! His death was an accident! An accident, I tell you! If I'd been thinking right, I never would've done it!" Lewis clutched his breathing tube so it would not dislodge, and coughed again. "Have you ever been overtaken by rage, Mr. Porter? If you have, then you know how crazy a person can get in a matter of seconds. You just go mad and do stupid things."

Lewis' words caused Jim Ed to stiffen up. Yes, he knew all too well that rage he was talking about. It had dominated so many years of his life, and Jim Ed also knew that under the right circumstances it could have been him instead of Lewis pleading for forgiveness. The only reason it was not was because of grace. It wasn't that Jim Ed was somehow a better man, but grace, pure and simple—the grace of God and of loving people surrounding him, encouraging him, praying for him—the grace of God's light shining upon him and the grace to recognize the truth before acting out. Something shifted in Jim Ed. He felt a measure of grace to release his anger and choose to forgive.

Jim Ed's eyes, now compassionate and warm, fell square onto Lewis'. "I forgive you," he said. "And I know God will forgive you too. The Bible says, 'The Lord is compassionate and gracious and does not treat us as our sins deserve. He knows how *we are formed. He remembers that we are dust.' Christ died for you too, Lewis." The moment those words came out of Jim Ed's mouth, Lewis exhaled as if a thousand-pound weight had been lifted from his back. "I believe Willie forgives you too," Jim Ed said, knowing in his soul it was true, that Willie would have, or had already, forgiven him.*

Tears still trickling down his face; with a wobbly hand, Lewis took Jim Ed's and squeezed. "Thank you," he said. "You will never know how much this means."

"I think I have an idea," said Jim Ed.

"I'm not sure how much time I have left on this earth, Mr. Porter," Lewis said, "a year, a month, perhaps only a few days, but I'm going to make the most of it. I want to find out what God would have of me and then do it."

"Just love the people God puts in your life, Lewis. Love them with the same grace that God has shown you." Jim Ed's words were few as he pushed Lewis toward his car. Lydia met them halfway. Jim Ed continued with them to the car, where they said a very stiff goodbye and Lewis was on his way. He died almost one month later.

21

"But what about justice?" I blurted out. "Lewis got away with murder, or at the least manslaughter! Shouldn't he be held responsible?"

"Yes, he should have. Forgiveness doesn't mean sweeping offenses under a rug and forgetting, nor does it means there will be no consequences," said Jim Ed, sitting back down on his stool. "It's a choice to release and let go. I'm not saying that justice is not important and should not be pursued. Thank God for justice and law. If there were no consequences to wrongdoing, then society would be even more chaotic. Yes, justice and sufficient punishment are essential. And it's important to grieve fully and feel the anger. However, people can get to the point where the anger and bitterness and the need for justice is enslaving and will destroy them and their relationships. Forgiveness, on the other hand, has little to do with justice and is as much for the person doing the forgiving as it is for the one needing forgiveness. Forgiveness is not only for murder, but everyday relationships."

"I'm not sure I totally agree. I mean, if somebody hurt my wife or kids I'd have a hard time forgiving. I'd want to kill them the way you wanted to kill Lewis, and I wouldn't be sorry either."

"If you feel that strongly, then you need to fight for them, Adam."

"Okay, that was tricky."

"No tricks. Just the Holy Spirit doing His thing, breathing life into dead spirits so they're no longer numb but passionate." He lifted his Saints cap and wiped his forehead. "Get back into the fight, Adam."

"That's what I want, Jim Ed," I said, "but what if I do this and Paige doesn't want to come back?"

"Sometimes you can't make things right or fix the mistakes you've made. I've learned too that you can't control other people. You can't control Paige's response. Stop keeping score."

The old painter's words were making me fidgety. I nervously pulled at the collar of my sweatshirt. He removed his glasses again and rubbed his nose with his thumb and index finger. "Remember I said that responding to God's light on the day when I was going to Lewis' was a defining moment for me?"

"Yes."

"I've discovered that life has many defining moments, places where we have to make choices of how we are going to respond—what voices we are going to listen to. Today is a defining moment for you, Adam, whether you are going to begin walking in the light and forgiveness. Are you going to get back into the fight, or are you simply going to continue on the same path getting the same results?"

22

Jim Ed stopped his painting and started cleaning his brush and palette.

"I guess that means you're finished?" I said, admittedly a little disappointed. I really didn't want our meeting to end. The sun had moved into the early afternoon position and I couldn't believe all that had transpired, how differently I felt from when we began.

"Yep, that should do it," he said, standing up from his stool. "You ready to take a look?"

"Can't wait," I said, stretching out my arms and legs.

"Close your eyes and grab my hand," he said. "I want you to get the full affect."

Feeling self-conscious, I closed my eyes while Jim Ed took my hand and guided me in front of the easel. Like a little kid presenting a beloved parent with some love-filled, handmade project, he wasn't the least bit uncomfortable.

"Okay," he beamed, "Open your eyes."

Looking down at the work of art before me, I blinked my eyes bewildered, and somewhat confused. Eric was right, the painting was nothing at all like I'd imagined. Wild, rough, and uneven, Jim Ed's masterpiece had numerous watercolor splotches and every square inch of the paper had paint on it. A jumble of colors, the images had borders that were non-distinct, blending into one another. At first glance it looked like a chaotic, elementary, finger painting. In the very center of the paper was my face. Jim Ed had done a good job capturing my likeness although it was still abstract, without fine detail.

Yet, there was something else even more bizarre about the painting. In addition to the image of my face located in the center of the paper, there were two smaller images of me. One over my left shoulder was an image of my face that was grayish and eerie, half-me, half-dragon, vicious, with scales and black, angry eyes. Over my right shoulder was another face of me yet it was in complete contrast to the dark one. Brilliant, bold, and peaceful, it was half-me and half-lion with striking eyes and a radiant, golden mane.

"So, what cha think?" Jim Ed asked, looking down with his hands on his waist.

"I...I...don't know quite what to say," I replied. "It's..."

"Different?"

"Exactly," I said. "I mean, it's certainly engaging and colorful. You're obviously gifted. But it's also dark and disturbing—not at all what I had pictured in my mind. I wasn't expecting three faces, nor for it to be so abstract."

"What'd you expect?" Jim Ed said grinning large and wide.

"I don't know," I said, "something more...what's the right word? Ummm..."

"Conventional?"

"Yeah, conventional."

"Now, Adam, do you really think I could ever do conventional? I'm an impressionist." Jim Ed let out a jovial laugh and slapped me on the back. "Let me explain the painting to you. It tells a story."

"Please do," I said. "I'm definitely curious. I was thinking more like, 'What is this?'"

"Like I told you, whenever I paint someone, I try to draw from more than just their exterior. I attempt to capture what their energy and soul are conveying to me."

"My soul was conveying to you that hideous dragon-like thing?" I was bracing for "Oh yes, that's you all right. You're a monster."

"Yep," said Jim Ed. "That's part of it, but it was also conveying to me the courage and spirit of the lion, the David in you that is struggling to come out and have a voice."

With my arms crossed over my chest, I was intently listening and studying my portrait thinking, *Okay, it could be worse,* when Jim Ed's cell phone dinged again. After checking the message's source, he handed the Blackberry to me. It was Josh.

"Where are you? I've been waiting forever! I'm going out with friends."

"Is Mom home?" I typed and pressed Send, then waited.

A few seconds later I got a reply. "No."

"Keep going," I said, handing the phone back to Jim Ed. "I need to hear what you have to say. A few more minutes won't make any difference."

"I believe God wants you to hear this too," Jim Ed continued. "I see this dark dragon inside of you, Adam. It's scary and loud and tries to control you. It's your flesh, your old nature. Sometimes it's so overwhelming that you feel paralyzed and want to give up on life and living. You're weary of doing the same things that you hate, over and over again. It's a cycle that reproduces itself and you don't know why. Inside you are tormented." He placed his arm on my shoulder and squeezed. "But I want to tell you something. Even though that dragon is powerful, even though it's loud and demanding, you don't have to let it rule you. You can slay it."

As Jim Ed spoke, something stirred inside me…hope, a fight that I hadn't felt for years. Something shifted. I wanted to slay the dragon. If there was going to be a fight, I was all in and was willing to go down swinging.

Jim Ed reached down and patted his old Bible. "You slay the dragon within you by using this—the Sword of Truth. The Word of God is *the* Light. It *is* your sword." I must have shown a look of slight hesitation, because he said, "Hear me out, Adam. This is important. It's going to change the way you see. The dragon, the enemy, is a deceiver. He likes to work in the dark, whisper lies in our ears like, *'You act like me. You look like me. You smell like me. God doesn't really love you. He's disappointed in you.'* The enemy is real. He's bent on destroying you and everything you stand for. You have to know the truth, know your true identity in Christ because when you mess up over and over again, that dragon will pop up its ugly head and start screaming, *'You don't belong to Christ. You're not even saved! Just give up on God and everything else. There's no use fighting the fight.'*

"But you can never give up the fight, Adam! The Bible says the kingdom suffers violence and the violent take it by force. If you're going to have a life, you have to fight for it. If you are going to have a family, you have to fight for it, and that fight starts by knowing the truth about yourself and about your enemy!"

Jim Ed shifted his attention to the lion face on the paper. "Now, you see this lion over here?" He said pointing, "This is what I see you becoming—what your inner man wants to become, finding true success and lasting contentment. So much of your identity has been wrapped up in performance. You've lost yourself, lost your voice. But don't be thinking it's too late for change and having a different life. That's another deception of the dragon. It's never too late until they put you in the grave. If anyone should know, it's me. The important thing in life is not how you start, but how you finish. Finish strong Adam, finish strong."

"I want to."

"Then never give up the fight! Fight for truth. The truth will set you free.

"The dragon within you feeds on deception. Deception is what hinders a person from letting go, walking in love, and receiving God's ever-flowing grace. As long as the dragon can keep you deceived, it can keep you in the dark, holding on to those ugly, self-defeating behaviors. It prevents us from trusting anyone. Keeps us from having the intimate relationships God created us to have. We were made in the image of perfect intimacy and our hearts long for this. But when you truly know who you are, that His spirit is in you, you recognize that certain self-defeating, even sinful, actions are not consistent with who you really are.

"Every time I've fallen short, Adam, it's been because I've taken my eyes off of who I am in Christ Jesus. Your identity is the key to outwardly becoming the masterpiece God created you to be. It's understanding that your spirit-man is already a masterpiece, Christ in you. Those who compromise are men and women who've become shortsighted or blinded by the enemy's deceptions and have forgotten who they are."

I stepped back, looked up into the sky, trying to absorb everything. Storm clouds appeared to be forming in the distance. I wondered if Paige was home now. "Looks like it's going to rain later," I said. "I might need to start heading on back soon."

"We could talk while we walk to the parking lot, if you don't mind," said Jim Ed. "My truck's there."

"That'll work."

At that, Jim Ed took my watercolor portrait, carefully rolled it up, slid it into one of his cylinders and handed it to me.

"Thanks," I said. "This is going to be a reminder to me—no more excuses."

"Thank you for allowing me the privilege of painting you." After saying that, he began putting away his paints then folded his easel and stool.

"I'm the one privileged."

Jim Ed took the handle of his cart and began to walk.

"Here, let me take that," I said gripping the cart to pull for him. He seemed spent.

"Thank you," he said. "Believe it or not, painting takes a lot out of me. I just don't have the energy that I used too."

The cart was surprisingly lightweight and we walked around the lake toward the parking lot as Jim Ed continued.

"Remember I said earlier that when you are secure in God and living in desperate dependence on Him, not in your own power or self-effort, the supernatural happens?"

I cocked my head. "Yeah."

"You receive healing from those past broken relationships and allow God to show you how to give your heart to the things that really matter. God's not broken, Adam."

"I want that," I said, letting out a deep, long sigh. "I've been sabotaging my relationship with my wife and my son, Jim Ed, going numb to protect myself."

"Kind of like Paige has done," he said.

23

"Fall is Paige's favorite time of the year," I said as we walked along noticing the beauty of the changing leaves. "Mine too. We used to like hiking through the woods taking in the beauty of nature."

"Leaves become their brightest right before they die, you know," he said. Some teenagers playing Frisbee sailed their disc our way, almost hitting the cart. It skidded to our feet. Jim Ed slowly bent down, holding his back with his hand and picked up the Frisbee and sailed it back wobbly to the kids.

At the parking lot, we walked to an extraordinarily clean, silver pickup truck with a matching camper shell. It could have been fifteen years old, but looked brand-new—definitely the kind of vehicle you wanted to buy secondhand. Jim Ed dropped down the tailgate and pulled out a ramp with rollers. Then he pulled down a cable that was connected to a small motor and hooked it to the cart. He turned on the little motor and it pulled the cart right into the back of the truck.

"I could have just put the cart up in there for you," I said.

"I know, but then you wouldn't have seen my contraption," he said. "It was my idea you know. As I got older, it became harder for me to lift stuff up in the truck so I developed this little baby."

"Clever," I said.

After closing the tailgate, Jim Ed shuffled to the driver's side door, opened it and slid in. Lowering the window, he rested his elbow in the opening. I tapped the cylinder holding my portrait in my hands. "Thanks for this, Jim Ed," I said. "I know I'm going to look at it and think about the things you've said."

He held out his hand and grasped mine, looked up at me, perhaps like a grandfather would. "God bless you, Adam Camp," he said. "It was nice meeting you. I pray you and Paige work it out and I pray Josh comes around."

"What do I do now?" I blurted out.

"Oh, I think you know," he said with a twinkle in his eye. Straightening his hat, he placed the key in the ignition, and cranked the engine. "See you later," he said giving me a quick military salute, while putting the truck into reverse.

I stood watching as the truck backed out of the parking spot and then began creeping forward. Standing there, holding the cylinder, listening to the gravel crunch under the truck's tires, I felt an unusual love for this man rising up in me. "Jim Ed, wait!" I shouted out, running toward his truck before he made it to the end of the parking lot. The old painter heard my shouts and stopped.

"Yes, Adam?"

"You can't...I mean, can we talk again sometime soon? Go for a walk or something? I know I'm going to need your help! There's so much I don't know, that I want to know, that I need to know. I feel like I've known you all my life and that you have more to teach me. Is there any way we could spend a little more time together, you know, be friends?"

Jim Ed looked at me with a twinkle in his eyes. "Like Jonathan and David?"

"Exactly!"

"I would be honored, Adam."

"That would be awesome," I said. "Can you write down your cell phone number for me and I'll give you a call sometime?"

He fumbled around for something to write on. Finally turning over an old gas receipt he scribbled down his number, folded the paper, and handed it to me.

"Thanks," I said. "I'll call soon."

Jim Ed tipped his New Orleans Saints cap once more and was off. My eyes followed his truck down the boulevard until it finally turned at a nearby intersection and disappeared into the early afternoon traffic. I glanced at the number and then stuffed the paper inside my jeans pocket.

24

With each step I took back through the neighborhood, the storm clouds grew closer causing me to hoof it, but it wasn't the storm on the outside I was worried about. It was the storm brewing inside me. The overwhelming peace I'd felt in the presence of Jim Ed was dwindling fast as the seriousness of my situation pounced back on me. *"I can't believe you actually fell for that heap of crap!"* the voice in my head jabbed. *"Really, an old eccentric painter? You're as crazy as he is. Nothing's going to change, Adam. You're not going to change. Get real. Paige is leaving you."*

A wave of nausea nearly knocked me over as the word D-I-V-O-R-C-E hovered in my mind's eye. It was a subject we'd never really brought up unless it was happening to someone else. Surely it wouldn't happen to us—not to me. Panting for air, my chest tightened as panic assaulted me. I bent over, bracing my hands on my knees and took in several deep breaths before moving on.

After turning the corner onto Sycamore Street, our house came into view and I noticed the garage door was open and the white Camry was gone. Josh's faded Honda Civic was in the driveway. *Paige is gone,* I thought. *It's been a couple hours, I guess I'm not surprised she didn't stick around for me. Josh must have been picked up by his friends. Good! The Civic's getting impounded!* The last thing we needed was a DUI or an accident on his record. He already had enough black marks to overcome.

A loud silence echoed through the house as I walked in. Normally, the quiet would've been a welcomed break, but now it just made everything seem hollow and empty. In the kitchen, I noticed the dishtowel Paige had been holding was still crumpled up on the table and the dishes were in the sink unfinished. Knowing her like I do it took a lot for her to walk away from unfinished dishes. She must have left right after me. I made my way straight to the master bedroom to get my iPhone off the dresser.

The door to the hall bathroom was cracked and the shower was running. Josh was home after all. Disregarding the fact that he had slept half the day and was just now getting showered, I stuck my head in. "I'm home," I said. No response. "I'm home," I said one more time. Still silence except for the trickling of water. *Fine, ignore me.* Seizing the opportunity, I rushed into Josh's bedroom, swiped up his keys, and continued to my room. It was an act that I knew would be equivalent to declaring War III but needed to be done.

Laying the canister holding Jim Ed's portrait on my bedroom dresser, I picked up my iPhone. There were only two messages, both from work. "Adam, we need you to come in this afternoon if at all possible. If not today, then early tomorrow. We found a problem with your report that needs to be resolved before we can issue on Monday. It's urgent!" The second message was a duplicate.

Problem with my report? I sighed, rolling my eyes. Well, there's the crisis.

"I'll be in tomorrow early to resolve," I typed and pressed Send. After that, I pulled up Paige's name and pressed call. I needed to talk to her, not text. I wanted her to hear my voice. Six or seven rings later, her voice message picked up. "This is Paige. I'm unable to talk right now but if you leave a message I'll get back to you. Thanks!"

"Paige, please, I need to talk to you. I said things I shouldn't have. Please listen. I'm sorry. I love you."

Within a minute I received a two word text. "Need space."

"How long?" I texted back while clanking around the room. Then I saw that she had packed some clothes.

"Don't know," she sent. "I've got some things to think through."

"What am I supposed to do about Josh?" I sent.

"You're his father. Handle it. I can't deal right now."

Now she wants me to handle it. I shook my head and plopped down on the bed. That figures. But if something goes wrong, guess who'll get the blame.

The sound of rummaging through the kitchen cabinets meant Josh was done with his shower and looking for food. Our house was nice, but still small enough for everyone to know everybody else's business, which in this case was in my favor.

Sitting on the bed waiting, anticipating the inevitable, I did not want to have *this* conversation with him. *Paige, where are you when I need you?* She helped balance me when dealing with Josh. The thought of her leaving was tearing me up. Another pain jabbed me in the chest. Paige, Josh, work—it was all closing in on me.

The pantry door closed loudly, then I heard Josh making his way back to his room like a large rodent where he closed his door securely, shutting me out and ignoring my presence. It occurred to me then that he probably had his headphones in the whole time and didn't even know I was home.

Pushing myself off the bed, I trudged to Josh's room. At the door, I vacillated between knocking it open and waiting it out a little longer. Just a few hours earlier I had wanted to put him in the ER. Now, I was numb again and rationalized that putting it off as long as possible was the way to go.

In the living room, I kicked back in my Lazy Boy chair with the remote. I just needed to chill for a while. The Vikings and Bears were playing in an important game with the Playoffs on the line. I'd planned on watching, but my life had taken a drastic turn. It's amazing how quickly things can spin out of control. 6:09 was left on the clock in the fourth quarter and the Vikings were on the Bears' eleven yard line about to score. The quarterback dropped back to pass and...and...the Bear's defensive coordinator had dialed up a blitz. The quarterback was going down. No! Wait! He scrambled out of the sack and found a man open at the goal line! Touch—

"Dad! Where are my keys?" Josh yelled out. "They were here when I went to take my shower!"

Okay, maybe he did know I was home.

I turned the TV volume up. "The touchdown is under review," the announcer said. "It appears the receiver stepped out of bounds on the one-foot line."

"Dad! I said 'Where are my keys?!'"

I pushed the off button on the remote and looked up. Josh now was standing in the living room in blue jeans with no shirt on, his long, wet hair shooting off in a thousand directions like he'd been drying it with a towel. Tall and lanky, at seventeen he'd gone through a recent growth spurt. I was six feet even. He was at least that tall, though I had about forty pounds on him.

"I have them," I said. "We have some things to talk about. I think you know what."

Josh rolled his eyes. "Whatever," he said.

"You don't think this is serious," I said, allowing my voice to elevate. "What's that on your arm?"

"Nothing," he said folding his arms over his chest.

I stood and marched over to him yanking his arms apart to reveal the words carved into his flesh, "NO PAIN" and "DIE." Red and freshly scabbing wounds; my stomach lurched as I inwardly groaned for my son and the damage he was inflicting upon himself. *Why would someone do that to themselves?* I thought.

"When did you do that?" I demanded.

"What does it matter? You weren't here anyway," he said, jerking his arms away from my grasp and flinging them in the air in protest. When he did, his fist smacked me in the mouth, busting my lip causing it to bleed. I think it shocked him because he braced himself for the retaliation. Though unintentional, the act tore at my self-control. "You're high!" I shouted clutching the back of one of his triceps, pulling him to me. "Let me see your eyes!"

"I'm not high," he yelled, pushing back away. "I need my keys. I've got to get out of here!"

"You're not going anywhere, punk! You shouldn't be driving in your condition and the car's in my name. I'm paying the insurance on it! It belongs to me. We are going to talk."

"Talking doesn't mean nuthin," he spat. "There's nothing to talk about."

"You can't keep using, Josh! Don't you understand? It's ruining your life. You're blowing it! You need serious help."

"I don't care."

"You don't care? How can you say that? On top of that, if you keep getting high, your butt's gonna wind up in jail—or worse you're going to hurt some innocent person! And if you do go to jail, I'm not bailing you out! That's for sure! I'm surprised you haven't been arrested already."

Josh just stood there glaring at me with cold, uncaring, eyes. He crossed his arms again, covering the scars.

"How many times have we been through this, Josh? If you have a record it's going to be hard to get into college. Now, you may not even graduate on time. You're smarter than this!"

"I'm not going to college anyway," he said nonchalantly.

"What!" I shouted, clenching my fists. "Well, if you don't—"

"What, Dad?" he said interrupting me. "I might not end up like you? If you're an example of success, no thanks! You're not happy! Mom's not. I heard you guys this morning. If the two of you can't make it, why should I even try? You ran her off and I'm leaving too! I don't want to be anything like you! Got it?"

With that, Josh bolted out the front door, slamming it behind him. I felt like I'd been kicked in the gut once again.

25

Bile rose up in the back of my throat and my hands trembled. I felt physically ill. *"Just look at you. You're a loser with a capital L,"* the voice berated. *"Josh nailed it. You drove both of them off. They're trying to get away from you. You drive everyone away. You've been doing it your whole life. It's a never-ending cycle."*

The panic and despair was now replaced with a suffocating depression that closed in around me...darkness like I was being buried alive. I considered plopping back down in the Lazy Boy and anesthetizing myself with football, but chose to limp back to my bedroom instead. Truth was I didn't know what to do with myself.

Back in my bedroom, I spotted the canister and slid my portrait out and unrolled it before me on the bed. The myriad of colors splashed and splotched with Jim Ed's impressionistic style once again leapt off the pages as my eyes scanned the images he'd captured. I compared the half-me, half-dragon with the half-me, half-lion. Which one was really me, the vicious monster or the courageous lion? There was no doubt in my mind. Then I noticed small letters written at bottom corner of the painting, something that I'd missed before. It was a Scripture reference. *Nehemiah 4:14.* I reached for a Bible that Paige kept in the bedside table and looked up the Scripture. *"Remember the Lord, great and awesome, and fight for your brethren, your sons, your daughters, your wives, and your houses."*

There sure has been fighting going on in the house, I thought, sliding the Bible back into the drawer. *I'm quite certain that's not the type of fighting Nehemiah was talking about.* Sitting there I felt the heaviness of my family, my home, my life crumbling down around me, and recalled the words of Jim Ed.

"I've discovered that life has many defining moments," he'd said, "places where we have to make choices of how we are going to respond—what voices we are going to listen to. Today is a defining moment for you, Adam, whether you are going to begin walking in the light and forgiveness; are you going to get back into the fight, or are you simply going to continue on the same path getting the same results?"

I was certain that if anything was going to turn around, something had to change—and that meant starting with me. I was the one who was going to have to take action. It was the only hope I had for saving myself and my family. In my mind, I knew all this, but my emotions were screaming just the opposite. The depression, fear, and regret now overshadowed any feelings of hope. All I felt was *hopelessness* and *despair*. Laying the painting aside, I curled up on the bed in the fetal position and rocked back and forth until I fell into a fretful sleep.

26

When my eyes popped open, my first thought was that someone had come in and pulled up the blinds because the late
afternoon sun was shining directly in my face. Squinting, I
instinctively shielded my eyes. Then it occurred to me that
the sun always sets on the other side of the house. Yet, if that
was the case, why was the whole room full of light, blinding
light, a light so bright my eyes should have melted in their
sockets? In fact, my whole body should have melted. I looked
down and realized that I had a different body, a new body,
one that absorbed the light. What was more amazing, however, was the light was alive and pulsating, moving in and
out of me, bathing me in inexpressible love and peace. Inside
the light, nothing else mattered. I was at peace, complete and
total peace. I didn't know where I was, but I never wanted
to leave.

Then I saw Him, a distinct figure stepping out from the
light, yet somehow *was* the light. Light was bursting from
inside Him and through Him. It was Jesus; I just knew that
it was. But this Jesus was unlike any being I'd ever seen
before. A magnificent blend of all races, His head and entire
body radiated with absolute holiness. The flames of His eyes
seared through to the deepest parts of my essence, revealing
everything true and repulsive about me. All that I'd tried
desperately to keep hidden in the dark corners of my soul was

exposed by the light and laid bare before the One who held the power of life itself in His hands.

At this knowledge, even though in a new body, I was repelled backward away from Him. "No! Jesus, no!" I cried. "I know what's in me. I'm not good. I've failed too many times! I'm so disgraceful. I'm unworthy."

"Oh, Adam, My son, I know you," Jesus said, His smile warm and comforting. When He spoke, His mouth never moved but I understood perfectly as the warmth of His love penetrated every atom of my being. "I know you better than anyone, better than you know yourself. I see you, Adam, all of you. I died for you. The price was paid. Your part is to receive My gift." He held out His hands, and that's when I saw the scars. For a moment, I remembered Josh's scars. Josh had cut himself out of frustration and pain, to experience some form of relief, but Jesus had allowed Himself to be excruciatingly tortured beyond anything our imaginations can fathom and then hung on the Cross because of me, because of my sin. Feeling the weight of how much pain I'd caused Him, I dropped to my knees and wept a river of tears, tears of gratitude.

"Adam," Jesus said, placing His hand on my shoulder, lifting me up. "I see you."

"Lord?" I trembled. "I don't understand."

"Look," He said. "I want to show you something."

In less than an instant, somehow I was outside my body, looking back at myself—the other me. I was clothed in a radiantly white, pure and shimmering garment fitted perfectly on my newly formed spiritual body. "This is the true you," said Jesus. "You are mine, Adam, clothed in My perfect righteousness. I purchased you with My own blood. See yourself as I see you. Live from your true identity, not your old man that is dying. You don't have to be a slave. My Spirit is in you to empower you to live the way I created you to. Only believe, Adam, and depend on Me."

Then I was back in my other body, looking in Jesus' eyes. He placed His hand on my shoulder. "Remember, I am with you always. You will experience troubles in the world, Adam, but have peace and don't lose heart because I have overcome the world."

Jesus began to fade back into the light around Him. "Wait!" I blurted out, sensing He was leaving. "What about Paige and Josh?"

"You will have all you need to do what is before you, for My Spirit is in you. I will comfort you and counsel you. Listen to My voice. Walk in step with My Spirit, Adam."

"Is Jim Ed an angel?" I impulsively asked. "Did You send him?"

"He's a chosen vessel, like you, Adam."

Just like that Jesus disappeared and I was left pondering the things He had said.

My eyes blinked open and I was still in the fetal position on the bed. A dream, I thought, yes, that was it—a dream! Yet somehow I knew in my heart what I'd experienced was more real than anything I'd known when I was awake. I slipped to my knees.

"Jesus!" I cried out. "Take me! Take what's left of my life and use it. Change me, God! Make me like You. Make me more like Jim Ed."

At that moment, it felt like warm oil poured over my head, covering my body and cleansing me from the inside out. That same overwhelming peace I felt in the dream was in the room. Jesus was here. It was as if I could see His blazing eyes, filled with warmth and compassion. He was so close. For a long time I knelt there beside my bed, weeping quietly, floating in His endless love.

Feeling another presence in the room, I turned around surprised to find Josh standing over me. At first, I wasn't sure what he was going to do, if he was going to cuss at me or take a swing, but then I saw the tears in his eyes. Our eyes linked and he fell down by my side collapsing into my arms.

"I love you, son," I cried, squeezing him tightly. "I love you so much!"

"I love you too, Dad," he cried.

I slid my arm around his shoulder like we were buddies, and we both sat there on the floor for a while. No words were spoken. No words were needed.

27

I unfolded the piece of paper with Jim Ed's number and entered it as a new contact in my phone. I really wanted to get with him and tell him my experience. I knew I couldn't tell just anyone. Some people would just write me off. I'd still not heard from Paige and had a gut feeling that dumping a new religious experience on her might make her leery. No, this was real. Something had happened inside me and I knew I would never be the same. Paige was going to have to see the new me. When the time was right, I would tell her.

Josh agreed to get into a professional program. We couldn't do anything until Monday anyway, and he didn't fight me any longer about the keys. Something had occurred between us. Josh wasn't bluffing, though I was perfectly aware that he could lie to my face with tears in his eyes. Yes, something real happened between us, but I knew it was going to be a long, difficult journey forward with him. I had a mixture of emotions running through my mind. I had to tell someone of my incredible experience so I entered in Jim Ed's number and pushed Call. I thought about Eric—he would just love this. Just like with Paige there was no answer, but this one went straight to voice mail after the first ring. "Jim Ed, this is Adam, something happened to me, man! Wonderful, strange, I've got to tell you. Can we meet? Call me."

For the next 20 minutes I paced the floor of our house, waiting. I finally gave up. Midway though a bowl of Captain Crunch Josh and I were having, my phone dinged indicating a message. I looked down thinking it was Paige, but it was Jim Ed.

"Meet me at the new McCafe at 6 pm," he sent. "The one at the corner of 101st street and Memorial Boulevard."

"Sounds great," I replied. "See you there."

I invited Josh to ride along with me to meet this painter dude and afterward get some pizza and hang out. I showed him the portrait that Jim Ed had done.

"Cool," Josh replied.

A block or so from the McCafe was the Forest Green Cemetery. As we passed by, I saw Jim Ed's truck weaving through the cemetery's main driveway out to Memorial Boulevard. Apparently he was leaving to meet us. I'm sure he didn't recognize us because he had never seen my vehicle before.

Josh and I pulled into the parking lot of McCafe and waited for Jim Ed. When he got out of the truck we walked to meet him in the parking lot.

"Jim Ed, this is my son, Josh," I said.

Wearing a black, long-sleeved t-shirt, Josh nodded. Jim Ed looked at him with his warm, inviting eyes and stuck out his hand. A big smile broke across his face. "Name is James Edward Porter. Friends call me Jim Ed. Nice to meet you, Josh."

Josh took his hand and shook it slightly. "I'm Josh."

Jim Ed tipped his Saints cap. "Fine young man," he said squeezing Josh's hand firmly. "Yes sir. You're bursting with intelligence and gifts. Can feel it."

Josh didn't speak, but his face lit up.

Jim Ed leaned in closer to Josh. "I see you, man," he whispered in his ear. "You're set apart for a divine purpose. God's got big plans for you."

As we walked in, I could tell Jim Ed was exhausted. He looked older and depleted, even more so than he had when we left the park.

After the three of us got our coffee and slid into our booth, Jim Ed turned to me and said, "So tell me about this strange and wonderful experience."

"Something incredible happened, Jim Ed!" I exploded, hardly able to contain my excitement, but trying to tone it down some. "I had a dream, but it was more than a dream. It was like a vision. I was in the light and Jesus came to me. He spoke to me. It was real Jim Ed, and I'm the last person to put stock in such nonsense as dreams!"

Jim Ed and Josh listened carefully, hanging on my words as I went into great detail.

"Somehow I'm different. It's hard to explain, but I feel it. I'm not the same person."

"Or you are just now understanding who you really are," added Jim Ed.

"Yes, I understand now," I said. "It's not about me, but Him."

Jim Ed looked at Josh, who was nervously picking at his arm through his sleeve. "What do you think about that story, Josh?"

"I know something happened to my dad," said Josh. "I believe him. He's never acted like this before."

"How 'bout another cup of coffee?" asked Jim Ed.

"Sounds good," I said and we all three got up and walked to the counter for a refill.

"Did somebody you know die?" Josh asked Jim Ed while we were waiting. "We saw your truck coming out the cemetery."

I shook my head, in an attempt to let Josh know we didn't want to go there, but Jim Ed interrupted me.

"It's fine," he said. "Yes Josh, somebody did die. It was my Christina."

"Who was Christina?"

"It's okay if you don't want to talk about it," I told Jim Ed.

"We need to talk about it, Adam," he said. "You need to hear it."

We sat back down at the booth and Jim Ed began.

"Christina passed from cancer not long ago, Josh," he said.

"How long?" Josh asked.

"Not quite eight months, but she was diagnosed a little over a year ago." He was trying hard to smile, but it was too much of a struggle so he gave up. "She'd been complaining of pains in her side and was getting more tired than usual, so we went in for a checkup. I was thinking it was probably just her age. You know, find the problem, get some meds, soon this thing will be behind us. That's what I was thinking. That's when the bomb fell. After the doctor poked on her side, he ordered a CAT scan. He said the tests would probably come back negative, not to worry. Three days later the phone rang. Christina had a mass on her spleen. The doctor explained that she had lymphoma, a cancer that attacks the lymphatic system of which the spleen is the center. It was aggressive and they gave her only months to live."

"I'm sorry," said Josh. "You can stop if you want."

Jim Ed just continued, dropping his head, talking into his coffee. "We hugged. We cried. Cried out to God. I felt emptiness and despair rising up inside me like cream in the milk bin back at our old dairy farm. The thought of going through even one day in this world without my Christina was more than I could handle. At home that night, after Christina was in bed asleep, I walked in the back yard and fell against a tree, gripping my face. My insides screamed. When I prayed, it seemed like God was slapping me down with a rod of silence. Where was God anyway? How could He allow this? Anger took root in me again, boiling up. I knew I was headed for another defining moment just like that day back in the truck when I was set on putting a bullet through Lewis' skull."

Josh's eyes about popped out of his head. "Putting a bullet through Lewis' skull?"

Jim Ed nodded, "Was I going to give in to despair and unbelief, let hate and anger rule me...or was I going to rise up and be a warrior for Christina during her time of greatest need? Maybe I was born for just such a time. This was not only Christina's greatest test, but mine too."

28

Her immune system down from the chemo, Christina had her worst week ever. For several nights, she lay in bed shivering violently for hours at a time with temperatures hovering at 104 degrees. A mere skeleton, she'd fall asleep then woke up enough to choke down a few swallows of Ensure, and then throw it up. It was horrible. Weak and frail, Christina was in pain almost continuously, even with pain killers. It was crushing Jim Ed to watch her. By then, Christina was too weak to pray out loud. She barely even talked. When she did it was only a faint whisper. Jim Ed, their son Will, and a plethora of friends had prayed for months believing God for a miracle healing or for the medical treatment to cure her, but things had only worsened. It appeared on the surface that God had taken a sabbatical.

"We can't give up," Jim Ed whispered into Christina's ear. "We have to draw strength from Him and keep going. He's here baby, He's here."

Sometimes he would encourage her by saying, "Christina, you're here on this bed doing the greatest work you've ever done for the kingdom of God. What you're doing now is as important as all the Bible studies you've taught, all the worship you've led, all the praying and witnessing you ever did. It's bringing together everything. This is your greatest work!"

Christina would nod weakly.

"By acknowledging God's goodness right here, in this situation, we're exalting Him and choosing to declare His glory before all of His enemies—before all His servants and all His creation! God is alive, Christina. You know that. You showed me that!"

She would nod in agreement.

"Christina because of your steadfast trust in our God, angels are bending low with furrowed brows. They're curious about you. And when they see your declaration of God's truth and faithfulness, they gaze in wonder and awe. All of God's enemies are watching us and gritting their teeth in frustration that they're not able to get us to doubt our God. They're looking in awe at you, Christina, and saying, 'Oh, what a great God she must serve if He was able to subdue her with the force of His love. What a wonder He must be.'"

In the hospital, during her worst stages—the urgency, the weariness, and the sheer awfulness of her lying there drove Jim Ed to a place of desperation he had never been to before. He made regular visits down to the hospital chapel to pour himself out privately to God.

"God, I feel so helpless!" he often cried. "Please, not Christina, God. Why her and not me? She's been so faithful to you! She loves you more than anyone I know!"

One night, disappointed and horror-struck, right there in that chapel, Jim Ed fell prostrate on the floor and wept until he had nothing left inside him but dry heaves and hoarseness. He didn't understand why God allowed Christina to suffer; and just when he felt he couldn't go on, God came down and met him there. He made a choice to stand by faith despite what the circumstances were screaming. He knew God was alive and he would trust Him. He would fight the good fight of faith.

Jim Ed didn't want to just grit his teeth and endure till it was over, so he determined to gather up everything that was good in the middle of the pain. God was preparing both he and Christina for something great in eternity. Yes, he wanted his Christina healed and for the pain to stop, but he didn't want to miss the work God was doing in the situation by being bowled over with what he hated. Jim Ed knew that cancer was evil and God didn't cause that hideous sickness, yet he also knew that God was working in the midst of it, in spite of it.

Late one night, Christina was in dire pain and he didn't know if she was going to live or die. They'd had a steady stream of visitors, and now Will and his family were gone. Jim Ed was pacing around the room, crying to God, "Lord, I praise You! We praise You! Christina, God's good. He's giving us grace and strength. Our Lord is right here with us."

She'd nodded and whispered a moan of agreement.

Christina had been getting a special medication for her blood that helped ease her discomfort. Unfortunately, the negative side effect was loss of eyesight. When Christina sensed that time was short, she refused the medication so her eyesight could be restored before she passed.

Day by day, hour by hour, Christina was weakening. The family knew the time was near. Her eyes were closed and Jim Ed, Will, and his family, and some close friends were gathered around her bed. Then, as if an angel cued them, they all began singing in unison. "Ama...zing grace how sweet the sound," their voices flowed out the hospital room and down through the hall, "that saved a wretch like meeeee. I once was lost but now am found, was blind, but now I seeeee." When they finished the chorus, everyone in the room, even the RN and nurse's aid, had wetness in their eyes.

At the end of the song, Christina's eyes barely slipped open. She turned her head, and holding her son Will's hand, she said, "I see you, son. I see you."

One by one those in the room kissed her forehead and said their goodbyes. When they were finished, she slowly turned to Jim Ed and lifted a trembling hand to caress his hair. "I see you, my love," she said.

With tears streaming down his cheeks, Jim Ed gently kissed her cheek and whispered into her ear, "It's okay, just let go and fly sweetheart. Go on and see Jesus and your Mama and Papa and Tallah. They're waiting. I'll be following shortly. And what a time it will be when we're all together again."

Jim Ed had crawled into bed with her and pulled himself up next to her back, helping her to stay warm. While holding her in his arms, he could tell her breathing was getting shallower and shallower. They both knew in their spirits it was time.

"Jim Ed," Christina said, mustering all of her strength, her voice crackly and faint, "Turn me around so I can see your face, I want to look into your eyes one last time." Her husband of nearly sixty years ever so carefully positioned her body to where she was facing him. They lay there facing each other.

Christina reached up her quivering hand and ran her fingers across Jim Ed's face while looking directly into his eyes. "I'm so glad that truck hit you that day, you old fool," she said barely above a whisper. "You're a good man, Jim Ed, and you've been a good husband. Thank you for standing by my side and being strong through all the hard times. And we sure had some good times too. Didn't we?" She smiled softly even though she was in pain. "If I could do it all over, I'd spend my life with you again. I love you so much." She wiped the tears from his eyes and then closed hers.

"I love you too, Christina," Jim Ed whispered back, gently stroking her silver hair. "You were the best wife a man could ever ask for. You made me a better man and filled my life with joy and richness. Thanks for loving me too."

Christina closed her eyes and laid her head back on the pillow. For the next several hours Jim Ed continued to hold Christina's hand as her heartbeat weakened. Will had moved to the bedside while his wife was asleep in the chair. Around 2 am, to their utter amazement, Christina's eyes popped wide open. She raised her head upright while gazing in wonder at something in the upper corner ceiling of the hospital room. A great smile filled her face. "It's time?" she asked. Then she closed her eyes, dropped her head back on the pillow, and breathed her last.

29

"I know she saw an angel or Tallah or her papa," said Jim Ed. "There's no other explanation. No way a person could be in that room and not trust God. Christina eyes opened because something called her. She opened them and looked straight up. She didn't even notice us."

"Or Jesus," said Josh, wiping tears from his eyes with his shirt sleeve. "Maybe she saw Jesus?"

"Yes, maybe she saw Jesus," said Jim Ed. "I know one thing for sure. God is real, Josh. Never forget that. He can break your addiction and help you achieve your purpose in life. If you give your life to Him, it won't be easy, but He will do great and wonderful things through you. I promise. You have so many special gifts to be developed. Don't let the enemy destroy you. But it takes courage to stand up against all the lies and deception that your generation is throwing at you."

"Yes sir. Thank you," said Josh.

"Know this," Jim Ed said turning his attention toward me again. "There's nothing more difficult than reaching over to Christina's side of the bed and realizing that no one is there. It hurts. I'd give anything to hold her in my arms just one more time. Those who love much, grieve much. But it's worth it, Adam. It's worth the fight. Your family's worth the fight."

I smiled, reached over and squeezed his hand. "Thank you, Jim Ed," I said. "Your story has moved me in so many different ways. I know Jesus sent you to me today."

"It's in these tough situations that we are given a chance to believe God is who He says He is," continued Jim Ed, "not because we are experiencing everything we want, but because we have a hope and we choose to believe. God is making you into something, Adam, and it's never too late to finish strong in life. Even in your darkest moments, if Christ dwells in you, there'll be a song deep in your soul and a warrior's fight in your swagger."

"Like David?" I said.

"Just like David," he said. "Hey Josh, can you Google Psalm 144:1 and 9?"

"No problem," Josh said and his fingers began flying on his iPhone. "Got it!"

"Read it out loud please," asked Jim Ed.

"Here's verse 1. *'Blessed be the Lord my Rock, Who trains my hands for war, and my fingers for battle.'*"

"You hear that? It's God who trains you for the fight. We're in a war, guys, and the enemy we're up against plays for keeps! Okay, now read verse 9."

"I will sing a new song to You, O God; on a harp of ten strings I will sing praises to You!"

"Although David was a mighty warrior who slew giants and conquered kingdoms, he also had a song in his heart for God." Jim Ed leaned back and took a long sip of coffee. "Do you mind looking up one more, Josh? Then I'll stop preaching. Promise."

"Sure."

"Look up Psalm 55:4-7."

"My heart is severely pained within me," Josh began reading out loud, *"and the terrors of death have fallen upon me. Fearfulness and trembling have come upon me, and horror has overwhelmed me. So I said, 'Oh, that I had wings like a dove! I would fly away and be at rest. Indeed, I would wander off, and remain in the wilderness.'"*

"Wow, I can sure relate to that," said Adam. "Felt that exact way this morning on that park bench. I wanted to escape to a beach in the Caribbean or just go to sleep and never wake up." I glanced at Josh. "I didn't really want to go to sleep and not wake up, son, they were just thoughts. I would never act on them."

Josh rolled his eyes. "I can relate to that Scripture," he said. "Who can't? Didn't know that was even in the Bible."

"Yep. You just read it." Jim Ed's eyes narrowed, he leaned forward over the table. "One thing I appreciate about God's Word is the honesty," he said. "People wouldn't make that stuff up. David was a warrior and had a song in his heart, but he also knew what deep pain and disappointment felt like. He had a very *real* life. Just because we are Christ's doesn't mean things are always going to be easy. But we will have assurance that in everything, good and bad, we can have a peace that passes all understanding, even when people misunderstand us or choose not to forgive."

"You mean like Paige?"

"Possibly."

"You have to give everything to God, Adam. Give it your best fight, His best fight rather, and leave the results up to Him."

"It's a hard thing, Jim Ed, but I hear you," I said glancing at Josh. "I love your mom, son."

"I know, Dad. I know."

There was a calm quiet around the booth for some time as we sipped our coffee simultaneously while dealing with our own thoughts. Then Josh looked up at Jim Ed, maybe a little hesitant. "Do you think you could paint my portrait too?" he asked. "You know, maybe sometime? When you don't have anything to do?"

Jim Ed perked up. His familiar smile beamed across his face again. "Now that is one of the best ideas I've heard all day!" he said with a twinkle in his eye. "I would consider it a privilege if you allowed me the honor of painting your portrait Josh Camp." He tipped his Saints cap then turned his attention toward me, eyes inviting.

"You can drop by the house anytime you like, Jim Ed," I said finishing off my cup of coffee. "And who knows...maybe sometime soon you could even paint a family portrait."

Acknowledgments:

The team at Destiny Image and Joel Nori—it's been a joy to work with you in this journey, and I sincerely appreciate your vision for this story.

Curtis Wallace, attorney and friend—thank you for believing in this project from the beginning and for bringing us together with Destiny Image Publishing.

Team Wildfire, Extraordinary Women, and AACC— your tireless and faithful service does not go unnoticed. Thank you for all you do for the cause of bringing healing and hope!

Julie, Megan & Ben, and Zach—you bring great joy to me as a husband and a father each day. I love my life with you!

Alanna Davis (Max's wife)—thank you for all your hard work on this book. Really, your name should be on the cover, too!

About the Authors

TIM CLINTON, Ed. D., is President of the nearly 50,000-member American Association of Christian Counselors (AACC), the largest and most diverse Christian counseling association in the world. He is Professor of Counseling and Pastoral Care, and Executive Director of the Center for Counseling and Family Studies at Liberty University. Licensed in Virginia as both a Professional Counselor (LPC) and Marriage and Family Therapist (LMFT), Tim now spends a majority of his time working with Christian leaders and professional athletes. He is recognized as a world leader in faith and mental health issues and has authored over 20 books including *Breakthrough: When to Give In, When to Push Back*. Most importantly, Tim has been married 33 years to his wife Julie and together they have two children, Megan (recently married to Ben Allison) and Zach. For more information, visit www.TimClinton.com and www.AACC.net.

MAX DAVIS holds degrees in Journalism and Biblical Studies. He is the author of over twenty books of both fiction and non-fiction. His books have been translated into several languages and have been featured on shows such as The 700 Club, The Today Show, and in USA Today. He and his wife Alanna live on thirty beautiful acres in Greenwell Springs, LA. To learn more, visit www.MaxDavisBooks.com.

MEN'S IMPACT WEEKEND
"WHERE MEN, GOD, LIFE AND THE OUTDOORS COME TOGETHER."

"Let us run the race marked out for us. Let us fix our eyes on Jesus, the author and perfecter of our faith." — Hebrews 12:1-2a

IMAGINE THOUSANDS of MEN, FATHERS, SONS, BROTHERS, SEEKERS AND CHRIST-FOLLOWERS coming together to WORSHIP GOD and learn more about the life of true adventure He intends for us as men.

Even more, imagine a two-day event packed full of WORKSHOPS, EXHIBITS, AND FUN around the stuff that men love: HUNTING, FISHING, FOOTBALL, MOTORCYCLES, RACING, EXTREME SPORTS AND OTHER OUTDOOR ACTIVITIES featuring some of the leading experts in the world.

Welcome to WILDFIRE WEEKEND FOR MEN! After years of perfecting our Men's Impact Weekend, we have landed on a unique format that helps men align their everyday passions with God's eternal purpose.

Think about some of the everyday challenges men face—a godless culture, fatherlessness, broken relationships, the porn epidemic and more....

It's time to ENGAGE men, CHALLENGE their hearts, and LEAD them into the adventure God created for them. Let's partner to lead men and transform generations.

WILDFIRE SPEAKERS PAST & PRESENT:

| TIM TEBOW | WILLIE ROBERTSON | JASE ROBERTSON | RICK HENDRICK | DREW BREES | ROBERT GRIFFIN, III | DARRELL WALTRIP | DEXTER MANLEY | PAT WILLIAMS | RANDALL CUNNINGHAM | JOE WHITE | BOBBY BOWDEN |

1.800.526.8673 ◆ WWW.WILDFIREWEEKEND.COM

 TWITTER @WILDFIREWEEKEND  FACEBOOK.COM/WILDFIREWEEKEND

INCLUDED IN MEMBERSHIP

Christian Counseling Today
Our flagship quarterly publication tackles the most pressing issues facing counselors and pastors. With its uniquely Christian point of view, *Christian Counseling Today* delves into today's hottest and most controversial subjects, offering analysis that is thought-provoking, clinically-excellent and biblically-sound.

Christian Counseling Connection
Our top-quality and recognized quality newsletter features professional reports and gives you the latest news, research and developments in the biblical counseling field. This succinct newsletter also features membership activities, promotes forthcoming conferences and addresses clinical, pastoral, lay, international and student issues.

Counsel CDs
This quarterly interview feature focuses on relevant topics in biblical counseling by experts in our field and is ready for your CD player when you have time for learning.

Presidential Insights
Join in on scheduled calls (quarterly), when AACC President, Dr. Tim Clinton, will discuss relevant topics and how they impact the current state of Christian counseling, as well as answer your questions.

AACC eNews
This monthly, Web-based electronic journal is geared to your needs and practice as a 21st century counselor providing up-to-the-minute news and views on important events and developments.

Member Discounts
Members receive registration discounts on popular conferences, as well as discounts on Continuing Education Credits, counseling resources, and books.

Counseling Resource Catalog
Recognized by the American Psychological Association, National Board for Certified Counselors, and most states. Through our conferences, publications and training programs, there are numerous opportunities available.

Opportunities for Continuing Education
Earn CE Credits through our conferences, webinars, publications and training programs with preferred pricing for members.

You will also receive a **Member Benefits Card** and **Certificate of Membership** suitable for framing.

Learn from today's most respected and influential Christian counseling and life coaching experts exclusively at...

LightUniversity
ONLINE

- BIBLICAL COUNSELING

- LIFE COACHING

- CRISIS & TRAUMA CARE

- CONTINUING EDUCATION AND PROFESSIONAL DEVELOPMENT

- PROFESSIONAL MEDIATION

... AND MORE!

Top 5 Reasons to Enroll in Light University Online:

▶ **1. LIVE YOUR DREAM... FOLLOW GOD'S CALLING IN YOUR LIFE**
Gain all of the crucial knowledge necessary to help others in need.

▶ **2. WORLD-CLASS FACULTY**
Our faculty includes 150 of today's most respected and influential Christian counselors, pastors and educators.

▶ **3. CONVENIENT AND FLEXIBLE**
Our innovative and easy-to-use online "Virtual Classroom" affords you the opportunity to study where you want. Plus, our terms start each month and our courses are only five weeks in length.

▶ **4. CREDIBLE**
Not only will you earn your certificate or diploma through Light University Online, but you also have the opportunity to earn college credit for your work or seek recognized credentialing.

▶ **5. AFFORDABLE**
Comparable programs would cost you at least double what you will pay at Light University Online... if not more.

ENDORSED BY: